MISSING

An Amish Mystery Book

Book 1

RUTH PRICE

&

SARAH CARMICHAEL

ISBN-10:1540413551
ISBN-13: 978-1540413550

TABLE OF CONTENTS

ACKNOWLEDGMENTS

All Praise first to the Almighty God who has given us this wonderful opportunity to share our words and stories with the world. Next, we have to thank our families, who support us through thick and then, even when we can be quite grumpy. Further, both Sarah and I have to thank my wonderful friends and associates with Global Grafx Press who support us in every way as a writers. Lastly, we wouldn't be able to do any of this without you, our readers. We hold you in our hearts and prayers and hope that you enjoy this book.

.

CHAPTER ONE

"Let not mercy and truth forsake thee: bind them about thy neck;
write them upon the table of thine heart."

Proverbs 3:3

>>Five Years Ago

Inside the kitchen of Andrew "Jumbo" Miller's Lancaster farm, kerosene lanterns sputtered as the sun crested the horizon in a sliver of orange. "Jumbo" Miller and his youngest son, Andrew "Beanpole" Miller, came into the kitchen on their way to the barn for their morning chores. Crisp air flowed in through the open windows, cooling the oppressive heat of the stove. Unfortunately, no amount of cool air could calm the temper of Jumbo's wife, Emma. She was in one of her "moods," slamming pots and pans on the stove as she battled her way through making breakfast.

Beanpole made the mistake of glancing up at her as he followed his *daed* to the barn.

"Why are you staring, boy?" Emma shouted. Her pupils were wide, and strands of her gray-brown hair had escaped their prayer *kapp* to create a distorted, smudgy halo around her face.

"Nothing," Beanpole mumbled and skedaddled out to help his *daed* with the morning chores. As father and son worked, Emma made breakfast, muttering to herself about the others in the community, "...and that little hussy Salome Beiler. She's not a Godly woman, showing off in her too tight to be Plain dresses as she works for that *Englischer*! My son is stupid for wanting to court her. She will drag him into a life of sin. Yes, she will..." On and on Emma went, muttering as she worked, slamming pots and pans onto the counters, which already showed chips and dents from her previous tempers.

In the barn, Beanpole worked carelessly through his chores. His mind was also on Salome Beiler. He daydreamed of holding her hand as they walked together after one of the Youth Sings. Thinking of the warmth of her skin against his made him wish for earthier things: the softness of her mouth, and their wedding night as he held her in his arms. Salome had refused all his offers so far to court with him, but she would come around. He was the best choice in their Amish community, and God wanted them to be together. He felt it with every beat of his heart.

"...then start planting...new seeds...Beanpole. Beanpole? Beanpole! *Andrew!*" Jumbo hated it when he was forced to shout to get into his son's private world. Why was he so absentminded? Jumbo worked very hard with his son to keep him grounded, but in spite of all of Jumbo's efforts, his son sometimes showed signs of being odd like his *mamm*.

Startled, Beanpole jumped up, spilling a good amount of feed onto the ground. "Wha—? Oh, uh, *ja*, that sounds *gutt*. I'll be happy to help you with the planting..."

"Beanpole! You weren't even listening to my plans for today! I told you we would be planting new seeds! When I speak, I want you to listen so we don't waste time! Now that it's getting cooler, you know it's the best time to get the fall planting into the ground."

Beanpole scowled, upset that he had been caught daydreaming by his *daed*, of all people. He despised the way his *daed* looked at him when that happened, as if there was something wrong with him. "Well, *Daed*, I'm sorry." He had worked hard to school his voice just right so none of the anger he felt would leak into his words. "I was thinking about our plans for today. I will be here to help you with the planting."

"*Gutt*. As ye sow, so shall ye reap, *ja*?" Jumbo clapped his son on the shoulder. "Now, let's get into the house and eat breakfast as quickly as we can so we can get to the sowing and reaping."

"Is *Mamm*...?"

"*Ja*, your *mamm* is in one of her moods again, and we don't want to make her angry." As he spoke, Jumbo rubbed one large hand over the fading bruise on his left cheek. Emma had left that on him several days earlier, when she had argued with him about the suitability of Salome Beiler.

Of course, Jumbo didn't want to see Andrew begin courting Salome either—but for an entirely different reason. Jumbo had long feared that his son carried the same mental instability that plagued Emma. He shivered and felt nauseated, thinking of the fears and horrors that Salome would experience if she courted or married his son.

Lord, I love my son! But if he suffers from the same illness that plagues my own wife, is it right to subject another innocent person to the emotional and physical abuse?

Jumbo had never tried to take Emma to be tested or treated to find what seemed to fuel her anger and abuse. Nor had he ever called the sheriff to his house. Along with other members of their community, he believed that they were equipped to deal with whatever happened. At the same time, he was beginning to question the wisdom of not relying on outsiders, especially since Emma's behaviors, words and actions had, yes, "tainted" their children. Every one of them seemed to have taken their *mamm's* issues into their own marriages, and Jumbo struggled with enormous guilt as he saw what his grandchildren had to deal with.

It will be fine. God will see that all is well. Jumbo told himself this, but as he looked upon his son, he wondered.

Jumbo forced his thoughts back to the present, clapping his large hand on his son's shoulder. "Breakfast, then work."

"*Ja, Daed*," Beanpole said, dutifully, but he had plans of his own. After breakfast, Beanpole promised his *daed* that he would meet him in the barn in a few minutes. It would be longer than that, but Beanpole figured his *daed* would forgive him once he learned Beanpole had secured a bride. "I'll be there. I just need to do one thing."

>>Present Day

Sitting in her kitchen, clutching her mug of coffee, Susie Zook shook her head, hopeful the gesture would shake away her sad memories. Five years ago, before she had married Joe, she had been Susie Yoder and her best friend, Salome Beiler, had suddenly gone missing. Where was she? Had she run off with an *Englischer* as some of the older women had suggested? Or had something more sinister happened?

Susie couldn't relinquish hold of the thread of hope that her best friend might return, even as each year made that possibility ever fainter.

Sighing, Susie stood up. Her belly was getting rounder, and she felt unbalanced as she went about her daily life. She walked slowly to the kitchen sink to wash her coffee mug.

As she did, the baby moved.

Her breath caught in her throat!

You're here!

The baby fluttered again, and then, just in case she'd doubted it, it gave Susie's insides a firm kick.

Susie's sad mood dissolved, overtaken with joy. "Ahh, *bobbeli*, you are making yourself known, finally!" Cradling her softly rounded belly with both hands, Susie closed her eyes and sent up a silent prayer of thanks. Even though she and Joe had been married for four years, this would be their first child. Susie had suffered two miscarriages, so her Amish midwife had insisted she go to receive full obstetrical care from a specialist in town. Wanting this pregnancy to result in a happy, healthy *bobbeli*, Joe and Susie agreed.

As though wakened from a stupor after the first movements, the baby kicked and cartwheeled through the morning, lifting Susie's mood as she went about her chores. It was warm outside and the birds chirped cheerfully in the trees. She cleaned the kitchen and then went upstairs to her quilting studio. Her baby's first quilt was spread in pieces in front of her, and now that the baby was moving, it felt more real.

Soon, you will be here!

Susie sorted through the fabrics—yellows, greens and blues.

She hummed hymns as she worked, sorting the quilt squares and sewing them together. As always when she was quilting, time flew by, and eventually the bright midday sun reminded her that it was time to get lunch together for her and Joe.

Folding the incomplete baby quilt back into the chest, she made her way to the kitchen, with a brief stop to relief her bladder. Now that this *bobbeli* had started to dance, she wondered if she'd ever have a moment's peace.

Well, no matter.

They would eat meatloaf, baked corn, broccoli and potato salad with leftover peach pie for dessert. She had just put the pie into the oven to warm when the front door opened.

"You're going to love your *daed*," Susie murmured to her baby as she closed the oven door. Then she shouted out to her husband, "Scrape your boots off on the mat! I don't want to have to mop this floor again."

"Yes, *mamm*."

Susie laughed. "Soon."

Joe strode into the kitchen, giving Susie a long kiss. When they had parted, both a bit breathless, he said, "Ahh, Susie, you look so bright today! What happened? Is it the *bobbeli*?"

"*Ja*! I felt the little one move for the first time! I was getting breakfast dishes done when he—or she—moved. And she hasn't stopped...or he? I know we shouldn't ask but...it hardly matters so long as the little one is healthy. Oh, Joe, I was so excited! I haven't been able to stop smiling since!"

Joe pressed his hand to his wife's belly. He loved to see his wife happy again as they approached the five-year anniversary of when Salome had run away—or vanished, depending on whom you asked. Memories of the disappearance had cast a shadow over Susie these past days. He worried about her and the stress her uncertainty might cause the baby. He wasn't sure Susie could handle losing another child. He wasn't sure he could either.

"Joe, are you okay?"

Joe forced a smile. "*Ja.* I'm just glad to see you're feeling happier." As soon as he said it, he wished he hadn't.

A shadow came over his wife's expression, and her smile dimmed. "I pray for Salome. I pray she is safe and that she is able to keep strong in her relationship with the Lord, if she can."

"I know. We all miss her. She was such a good friend to so many of us."

"I just wish I knew what happened to her! If she ran off with an *Englischer*, she would have sent a letter at least!"

"Jumbo Miller saw her getting into a car with an *Englischer*."

"I don't believe that."

"You know Salome was always a bit wild."

"Not that kind of wild. And Jumbo..."

"He's an honest man—upstanding."

"*Ja.*" Susie sighed. "I just wonder why Salome never said anything about leaving that day. She never even gave me a hint. I dropped her at Mrs. Ashton's house at seven that morning and told her I would be there before five that night with the buggy so we could go to the Sing. Salome was excited about the Sing, or seemed like she was at least. But when I came back... It is odd, isn't it? She just vanished without a trace."

"Not without a trace. She was picked up in a station wagon. Mrs. Ashton saw it tearing down the road like the devil himself was on its heels."

"I know." And Susie might doubt Jumbo Miller's honesty, what with his wife being so odd and his making so many excuses for her, but Mrs. Ashton was the sort who would give a cashier back a penny if she'd gotten a penny too much in change. "It just hurts that Salome didn't feel that she could trust me. If she wanted to go, I'd have understood, and we'd still be friends. We still are friends."

"I know, Susie. I know."

"I paid for an advertisement in the Amish paper, just in case someone had seen her."

"If someone doesn't want to be found, you won't find

them."

"But what if that *Englischer* did something?" Tears streamed down Susie's face.

"Ahh, my love, my sweet! Cry, just keep remembering her with all the love you felt for her then." Joe enclosed Susie's slender form into his arms, cradling her against his broad chest.

Susie took his advice, crying herself dry. Eventually, she raised her head from Joe's chest. "*Ach!* Your shirt…it's all wet and sticky. Go upstairs and take it off. Throw that one into the wash pile right now!"

"*Ne*, it's only your tears. That is much more pleasant than a day's built-up sweat. Let me bring the meat to the table."

After lunch, Joe went back to work. Susie finished the tidying up, leaving her kitchen sparkling clean. Bringing her light cloak with her, just in case it got cold, she went into the barn to hitch the horse to her buggy.

If Joe had been there, he'd have forbidden her from doing it, afraid for the baby, but Susie was more practical. Her *Englisch* doctor was confident that the baby was healthy, and while the little one was sleeping now, after the acrobatics performance that morning, she was confident her *bobbeli* was hale and hearty. And the warm autumn air would do them both some good.

On her way, though, she stopped at Joe's *daed*'s carpentry shop. His farm bordered their own, which allowed Joe to walk to work and home for lunch. She tied the horse up and peeped in the door, the sweet smell of cut wood caressing her nose. "Joe. I'm going to buy some quilting supplies." After Salome's disappearance, Susie had always been careful to tell someone where she was going before she left her home.

Joe looked up from a chair leg he'd been sanding with a horrified expression. "Susie! Why did you do up the buggy on your own? I'd have come home and—"

"I'm pregnant, not an invalid, Joe. And I should be back by mid-afternoon."

Joe's *daed* laughed, and Joe at least had the grace to look a bit sheepish. "*Ja*, I mean..."

"I love you, husband," Susie said, "and you too, *daed*," she added, waving at her father-in-law.

***

She had just finished loading up her groceries when the *bobbeli* woke up and gave Susie a firm kick in her bladder.

"*Bobbeli!*" Susie exclaimed, touching her stomach. There was such a thing as too much of a good thing.

"Are you alright, hon?" A woman in a bright flowered dress and white linen shirt came over to Susie. She was light brown with thick, corkscrew curls. She touched her stomach, which Susie realized was also large. "When are you due?"

"December."

"January," the woman said. "I'm Tiffany. Yours looks like a kicker."

"*Ja.*" Susie sighed. "I mean, I'm blessed, truly blessed. All I want is a healthy little *bobbeli*. Baby…it means baby."

Tiffany smiled, "I figured as much. Is this your buggy?"

"*Ja.*"

"I can keep an eye on it while you find yourself a bathroom."

"Danki!"

"Us mamas have to stick together." She held out her hand to Star, Susie's horse.

"Star," Susie said, pointing at the diamond of white fur between his eyes. "I know it's a diamond but—"

Tiffany laughed. "I understand. We grew up with a brown tabby cat named Pumpkin because my little sister got her around Halloween."

Susie smiled, "Star likes carrots." She leaned in to the back of the buggy and pulled out a carrot from the topmost bag. "Just give her this and she'll be your best friend."

"I've always loved horses," Tiffany said with a wave. "Go ahead. We're all good here."

Susie was grateful. Not that she expected anyone would

steal from her buggy, but it felt good to know someone was watching. If only to make sure she didn't disappear.

Since Salome had vanished...left, Susie hadn't been able to erase the irrational fear that one day she, too, might come up missing. Would everyone just assume she'd run off, and then go on with their lives?

No, Salome hadn't vanished. She'd gotten into a car with some *Englischers*. She'd run away.

Susie's buggy was parked in front of the fabric store, so she dashed inside the store to freshen up. The *bobbeli* was twirling, and Susie knew that if she didn't relieve her bladder here, she'd be stuck making a pit stop along the road. Inside the fabric store, a light lilac smell filled the air, which was also a good bit cooler than the air outside was. Susie closed her eyes for a moment and let the air conditioning wash over her. Sure, it was against the Ordnung to have it in their homes, but that didn't mean she couldn't enjoy a little...

Her gaze passed over the inside of the store. Fabric rolls were stacked up on shelves with some leaning against the walls. A cutting table stood in the back of the store next to the register. One of the new girls, a chubby high schooler named Janie, stood behind the cutting table talking to...was that Beanpole Miller?

Beanpole was still true to his nickname: he was tall and rangy with hair like a scarecrow. A chill passed over Susie. It was uncharitable, but Beanpole had always made her uncomfortable. His emotions always seemed a bit off. He was too serious when everyone else was laughing, while smiling brightly when others were serious. He'd made Salome nervous too. She'd mentioned how he seemed to stare at her a lot at the youth sport gatherings. Susie hadn't noticed, but she'd been too busy watching Joe. Now she felt like she'd betrayed her friend.

Beanpole leaned over the counter pointing at a strip of rich red ribbon.

Susie's chest tightened with fear. Salome had always said if she was an *Englischer*, she'd wear red ribbons in her hair. Susie watched as Janie pulled a foot of ribbon and cut it.

"One more," Beanpole said.

Janie laid the second strip of ribbon onto the table.

"Excuse me?" Susie asked. "May I use your ladies room?"

"Of course!" Janie tapped at the register, which clicked as she tapped at the numbers. "Over there, next to the chiffon."

Susie forced a smile. "Beanpole," she said with a nod. She wasn't happy to see him, so she didn't say that. It was a sin to lie.

He nodded to her but didn't return the smile.

"Is that ribbon for your *mamm*?" Susie asked.

"*Ne.*"

Janie handed him his change and a small paper bag with the

ribbon inside. He said, "Danki," and picked up the bag. With no further explanation, he left.

Susie hurried up through the ladies room. She hated to leave Tiffany so long with her horse and groceries but the ribbon, and Beanpole's behavior about it, worried her. She walked over to the desk where Janie was now hunched over, tapping on an *Englisch* cellular phone.

"Janie?"

Janie looked up. "Yes," she blurted out with an edge of panic in her voice. "Can I help you?"

"Does Beanpole buy ribbon a lot here?"

"Beanpole?"

"The guy who just left."

"Oh, him, nah. Maybe twice this past month. He said he used to go down to Gloria's in another town, but they went out of business."

Gloria's was at least an hour away by buggy. "That's odd," Susie said. "You're much closer to where we live."

Janie shrugged. "I guess. Can I get you anything, ma'am?"

"No. No thank you."

When Susie got back to her wagon, Tiffany was standing next to Star, petting the horse's neck. "Thank you so much!" Susie said.

"Your Star is a sweetie!" Tiffany said. "I always wanted to have a pony, but we grew up in the city. I told my mom we could keep her in the back yard, but..." Tiffany shook her head with a laugh. "I got a bicycle."

"Do you live around here?"

"Malcolm and I moved out to Lancaster a couple of months ago. I wanted my baby to grow up in the sunshine. I admit though, it's tough getting used to small town life. It's so dark at night, and there are so many crickets. You think it wouldn't bother me after the ambulances and cop cars, not to mention the bus that used to go by our house, but..." She shrugged. "I'm getting used to it. Where do you live? Maybe we could get together sometime. Talk about mom stuff." Tiffany sounded a bit wistful, and Susie realized that she was probably lonely. "If that's not, like, against your religion."

Susie laughed. "We can have whatever friends we want. It's fine. Why don't you and Malcolm join Joe and me for dinner sometime?"

"That would be great." She reached into her purse and pulled out a cellular phone. "Let me give you my num— Umm...how do I reach you?"

Susie laughed. "Can you write down a phone number? My husband's *daed* has a phone for his carpentry business. He also has email, but it's for business only. You can call though and leave a message. I'll call you back."

"That sounds great!"

They exchanged phone numbers and an awkward hug, more on Tiffany's end, before Susie scrambled up into the buggy.

As she directed Star back onto the road though, she couldn't help thinking about Beanpole and the red ribbon.

CHAPTER TWO

>> Nine Years Ago

"If I was to become an *Englischer*, Suz, I'd always wear red ribbons in my hair!"

"Isn't that a bit childish?"

Salome shrugged. "I think it's pretty. Braids and ribbons, like this doll I saw in a store window in town. I mean, there's nothing wrong with being Plain, but don't you want to have a little fun sometimes? Maybe try some lipstick? You'd look good in purple with your blonde hair."

Susie laughed, her face heating up. "Like when we picked all of those blackberries. Your *mamm* was furious. She said she'd never get the stains out of our aprons."

"When I go on *rumspringa*, I'm going to wear lipstick and red ribbons every day."

"I want to see a movie," Susie said, excitement overtaking her as she thought of her future. "Captain America. There was an advertisement for it on the last page of one of my brother's comics."

Salome breathed through her teeth. "You're so lucky your brother lets you read his comics."

"Just the old ones. I'll get you a copy."

"*Ne*, my *daed* would flip." Salome's expression darkened and Susie knew better than to press the issue. Sometimes, when they were younger and still in school, Salome would come in with bruises on her arms and back. She never said where they came from, but Susie knew her *daed* beat her and her *mamm* when he got his hands on spirits.

Drinking was against the Ordnung, but Salome had begged Susie not to say anything, or they'd all have to move back to Elkhart to live with their *mamm*'s *mamm*. Susie never wanted her best friend to leave, so she kept her mouth shut. Besides, everyone knew that Salome's *daed* was strict and believed more in the rod than spoiling the child.

"Well," Susie promised, "I'll bring a whole stack of comics next time we go berrying."

"*Danki!*" Salome's voice caught. She was smiling, but her eyes shone as if she wanted to cry. She took Susie's hands and squeezed them tight. "You're my best friend. When we go away on our *rumspringa*, we'll have real adventures, I promise."

Susie nodded, but she wasn't really sure if she wanted to go away on her *rumspringa*. She and her *mamm* had been visiting their classmate Joe's sick grandma, helping her around the house, and Susie had found herself growing closer to Joe. Not kissing close, but friend close. He made her feel special when they were together, and she wondered, when they were old enough, if he might want to court with her.

"We're going to have the best *rumspringa*!" Salome said. "I can't wait! As soon as I'm old enough, I'm getting a job and getting out of here, if it kills me."

>> Present Day

The next week, driving from town to her home, Susie spotted Beanpole walking ahead of her on the side of the road. In his right hand, he had a small paper bag. *More ribbon?* It had to be. He gripped the bag tightly, crumpling the paper at the top.

Susie slowed Star, wanting to see where he was going. He looked up. "Susie Yoder?"

"Zook now." She and Joe had been married for almost four years. How had he forgotten? Maybe he really was a little off...like his *mamm*. "Are you heading home?"

"*Ja.*"

"Shopping for your *mamm*?"

"*Ne.*"

Having a conversation with Beanpole was like pulling teeth out of a cow's jaw. Susie considered offering him a ride, but it was against the Ordnung for her to be alone with a man who was not a family member or her husband. Not that she wanted to share a wagon with Beanpole Miller. The thought made her stomach sick. "Well, have a good afternoon," Susie said.

As Star pulled her buggy past Beanpole, she glanced in the rearview mirror. He walked, gaze fixed forward, and for a frightening moment, Susie felt as if he was watching her. The road made a shallow right turn, and in the rearview mirror she saw him stop, his arms folded over his chest. The bag was still gripped tightly in his right hand. He looked as if he was waiting for someone.

Susie let Star walk for another minute, but she couldn't shake the feeling that something was wrong. So when the road widened, she looked both ways and then directed Star in a U-turn. But when she'd reached the place where Beanpole had been standing, he was gone.

Her heart caught in her throat. And then she thought about it for a few seconds and kicked herself as she looked over the field. His *daed*'s farm was that way. On foot, all he had to do was cut through the gap in the fields on her left, and then he'd cut at least fifteen minutes off his walk home.

He's just gone home, stupid.

Still, as Susie looked out over the field with its new growth, she couldn't see him. He was probably behind one of the trees in Mrs. Stoltzfus' apple grove. Or on the other side of her house even, if he walked quickly.

Susie looked to the opposite side of the road. That land was untended, a thick mass of trees and hedge that looked undisturbed. Wasn't that the way to Widow Trudy's old house? Susie's *mamm* had always called it a crying shame that the widow's son had left the house behind like an unwanted child. If someone had passed through, branches would be broken and the dirt would be disturbed.

No, he'd gone home. Probably his *mamm* wanted something with the ribbons, maybe for a quilt commission. Some *Englischers* liked those kinds of frilly extras, even if it wasn't really in an authentic Amish style.

Susie shook her head. Maybe it was her hormones that had her feeling so suspicious. Her *Englisch* doctor had warned her about that. Or maybe it was just that Beanpole had always unsettled her. But that didn't mean that she had a right to be chasing after him. And if he was up to something, Heaven forbid, what was she, a pregnant woman by herself on a roadside, going to do about it?

Susie turned her buggy back around and continued home. Still, as much as she tried to tell herself that she needed to put her suspicions about Beanpole to rest, she couldn't shake the ribbons. Two feet were hardly enough for a quilt.

At home, Joe helped her unload her supplies. Something of her worries must have shown on her face because as they took the last bag up onto the porch, he asked her, "What's wrong?"

"Do you talk to Beanpole Miller at all?"

"Beanpole? *Ne*." Joe shrugged. "He's always been a bit odd. Especially when all the rest of us started getting married and the girl he was courting with ran off on him."

This was news to Susie. "What girl?"

"I don't know. Someone from Ephrata I think. They met at an *Englisch* party, or at least that's what he always said. I figured he was making it all up because he couldn't get any of the local girls to look at him twice."

"He scared Salome."

"*Ja*, he used to talk about wanting to court with her all the time, but then she went off with those *Englischers*."

"So, the girl he was courting with ran off at the same time as Salome?"

Joe blinked, his gaze darting upward as he thought about it. "*Ne*, he took up with the other girl after Salome left. That's when he started skipping our Sings to go off to Ephrata. Or at least that's what he told people. Lying's a sin, but Beanpole never much minded."

"He's taken his Kneeling Vow!"

"*Ja*, he has. And he comes to Church. Why are you asking about Beanpole?"

"It's probably just my hormones acting up."

"Susie, you're not posed to flights of fancy. Something about Beanpole has you worried. What is it?"

Susie took a breath. She and her husband had chosen to share their lives, and they were bringing a child into the world. If she trusted him enough to share her life with him, she could trust that he wouldn't judge her for her suspicions. "I saw Beanpole last week at the fabric store. You know, when I met Tiffany who's coming for dinner on Thursday?"

"*Ja*."

"Well, Salome always loved red ribbons," Susie detailed everything that had happened: his purchase, his odd answers, and today, how he had frightened her on the road. As she laid the evidence out, it seemed so vague. Almost like gossip, and Susie felt ashamed. "I shouldn't be judging him just because he buys some ribbon, I know."

"You shouldn't have gone back by yourself," Joe said. He took her by both hands, holding them a bit too tightly.

"So you think there's something to it?"

"*Ne*...I don't know. The *Englisch* police investigated—"

"But since Salome was a legal adult, and Jumbo testified that she'd gone off with those *Englischers*, they didn't do much. But she hadn't packed anything. Not even her comics. I told the officer that, but..." Susie swallowed. Her throat felt thick with grief, fear, and years of smothered suspicions. "I don't think Salome ran off. I think something happened to her. And I think Beanpole knows something about it."

"Stay away from Beanpole."

"If you think he might have done something to Salome, we have to find out."

"You are my wife, and you are carrying our child." Joe was yelling at this point, and his grip on her hands had become painful.

"Joe, you're hurting me!"

He let go of her hands as if they had burned him. "I'm sorry, Susie, I'd never hurt you." His face was red, and he wouldn't even meet her gaze.

Susie walked to him and put her arms around his waist. "I know." She kissed his jaw. Her cheeks were wet. "I know you wouldn't. I love you, Joe. We promised forever, and that's all I want."

Some of his ramrod stiffness eased. He leaned down and cupped the side of her jaw in his palm as if she were made of glass. "I'll talk to Beanpole, okay? If he is up to something, I don't want you mixed up in it. But I'll talk to him."

She closed her eyes and let him kiss her. It was warm and

sweet and, for the first time since she'd seen Beanpole Miller walking alongside the road ahead of her, she felt safe.

CHAPTER THREE

>> Five Years Ago

Susie Yoder sang snatches of pop music she'd heard in a store in town to herself as she drove her buggy to pick up her best friend for the Sing that evening. She wasn't as good a singer as Salome was. Her friend's rich alto caught the ears and attention of everyone who listened. But Susie didn't have to catch everyone's attention. She only had to capture Joe Zook's interest, and since they'd spent ten minutes talking together on a picnic blanket after Church last Sunday, Susie was pretty hopeful that she had a chance.

She turned her buggy up the circular front drive of Mildred Ashton's home. It was three stories tall, a stately matron painted white with egg-yolk yellow trim around the windows. Susie tied the horse up in front of the house and walked up the stairs onto the porch to ring the doorbell. It surprised her that Salome wasn't just sitting on the porch, waiting as usual. The door swung open and Mrs. Ashton greeted her, eyes alight with fury. Susie was shocked.

"Miss Yoder, is it?" Mrs. Ashton barreled forward without giving Susie a moment to breathe, let alone answer. "Your friend's run off."

Mrs. Ashton was tall and thin with gnarled hands and manicured nails that were always perfectly polished in either gold or pink. Today it was gold. Though Mrs. Ashton rarely had company, Susie had never seen her in nightclothes. Instead, she dressed for the high-powered job she'd held in the city a decade ago. Today she wore a perfectly pressed gray skirt, maroon blouse, pearl earrings and matching bracelet and, of course, her wedding and engagement ring glittering on her left hand.

Susie was shocked. "What do you mean? Ran off where?"

"Don't know. I called and I called for Salome, but she didn't come out. And then I had to get up out of my bed with my aching joints and search up and down this house to see if the fool girl had gotten herself into any trouble. She's run off. Took her jacket and is gone. Tell her when she comes back that she's fired."

"Salome wouldn't just run off like that!"

"Would and did. Right after she went downstairs to put the wash in, but before I knew she'd run off, I heard a car tearing down the road," Mrs. Ashton pointed down the driveway to the road that passed her home. "The thing was beeping and kicking up so much noise, I stood up to get a better look. It was one of those station wagons. I always hire you Amish girls because you're so honest, but Salome, she was sneaking around using my phone when she thought I was asleep. I know it was to talk to her friends. You know, the non-Amish ones. Maybe you can ask some of them."

Non-Amish friends? Susie was suddenly hurt. Salome had non-Amish friends, but had never mentioned them? And now she had taken off with them, abandoning her work and her best friend without a word?

No, Salome would have said something. "I don't think she ran away," Susie said. "Maybe someone in that car took her."

"Why would they do that?"

Susie shook her head. "I don't know. But it can't be good. Can we call the police?"

"Your friend's not going to appreciate it if you have the police hunting her down when she's just trying to have herself some young people fun."

Susie couldn't say Salome wasn't the type to 'have young people fun', but she'd have said something—maybe invited Susie along. No, a grim certainty settled itself in Susie's mind. Salome needed help. She said, "We should call the police."

"Yes, well, I had been thinking if you came back around that you might let me know if making a call would be necessary."

"When did you last see her?"

"Well, that car interrupted me in the middle of my nap, and the machine was still going when I went downstairs, so she couldn't have run off more than an hour ago, maybe an hour and a half."

An hour… A lot could happen in an hour. Mrs. Ashton led Susie to her kitchen to make the call. A rotary phone hung on the wall. She pushed a gold-painted nail into the hole above the nine and pushed it in a clicking circle. After repeating the motion in two short movements for the one, she held the phone up to her ear and waited. "Yes, is this the police? The girl who works for me has gone missing. Yes. I thought she'd run off, but her friend's worried something might have happened. Yes. Yes, we'll make a statement. She's Amish. Uh-huh. Thank you, officer." She hung up. "They said they'd send someone over."

For the next half-hour, Susie sat on the edge of Mrs. Ashton's plastic-covered sofa and waited as her stomach twisted itself into knots.

She wouldn't stop waiting. As the years passed, even as her life moved forward, a part of her stayed perched on that faded ivory brocade sofa, slipping forward and shifting back on the thick plastic covering as she prayed, in vain, for her friend to return.

>> **Present Day**

That night, Susie stood by her kitchen window. Though the temperature was warm, a prickle of fear raced along her skin. Shivering, she dropped the sheer drape and hurried away from the window, bumping into Joe.

"Whoa!" He steadied her. "Are you okay?"

"I'm—" She couldn't say fine because she wasn't, so instead she changed the subject. "How about some hot cocoa? I'm feeling chilly."

Joe looked confused. It was almost sixty degrees outside, but he nodded. "With whipped cream?" he asked.

Susie laughed. "You can have some if you want, but I don't want to get too heavy."

Joe heard the hollowness of Susie's laugh. Running his hands up and down her arms, he gazed softly at her. "Memories?"

"Ugh, *ja*. I feel creeped out. I was sitting by the window, just remembering. When I looked out, I felt as though someone was looking in."

Hearing this, Joe shivered. "You stay here. Heat the milk while I look outside." Grabbing his coat, he strode to the front door.

"Joe, be careful! Please!"

Joe looked back with his hand on the doorknob. "*Ja*, I will." Grabbing the house key from the wall, he locked the front door as he stepped outside.

Susie regretted saying anything. Hugging herself, she stood in front of the stove, stirring the milk. Even the baby was still. It felt like forever, but Susie knew that Joe was probably only outside for a few minutes. Hearing the familiar thump of his foot on the porch, she poured the steaming milk into twin mugs.

Where was the cocoa?

Joe walked in, and she let out an audible breath. "Did you see anything?"

"*Ne*, I did hear something, though. It was moving around in the bushes, but it was gone when I got over there."

Susie gasped. "Do you think…?"

"That Beanpole's out there? *Ne*, it's probably a raccoon."

"*Ja*." Susie laughed. "I feel so foolish. We live in a safe community, and I've known Beanpole since we were both children in school."

"You never can really know someone. I'll talk to Beanpole at our next Church meeting and get things sorted out."

Knowing that Joe supported her in spite of the vagueness of her fears meant the world to Susie. She finished preparing the cocoa, putting a large dollop of whipped cream on top of Joe's cup before handing it over. They sat together at the kitchen table, sipping cocoa while the baby fluttered in its sleep. When they'd finished, Susie walked over to the sink and rinsed out both of the cups.

Suddenly, from the direction of the barn, there came a loud crash.

Joe leapt to his feet. "Sit down," he said. "I'll get the shovel and scare it off."

Raccoons… It had to be a raccoon, messing with the trash. But the compost was on the other side of the house. "I should come with you," Susie said.

"*Ne,* stay put."

Joe walked out again. Though he had asked her to stay in the kitchen, anxiety swirled through her and she couldn't stay still. Taking up a lantern, she walked down the hallway to the dining room which had a good view of the barn.

Joe was a stocky shadow as he approached the barn door. It was open, swinging, and Star had run out onto the field. The pair of buckets for watering and feeding Star had been kicked into the barn door. Joe walked into the barn, and a few seconds later a glow came from inside where he had lit one of the lanterns. A few minutes later, he came out and called for Star.

Susie's heart settled as Joe led Star back into the barn and closed the door behind him. When Joe returned, Susie met him at the door, where he was scraping his boots on the mat. His face had a grim expression. "There's no way that door was opened by a raccoon," he said.

"Do you think it was Beanpole?"

"I don't know. But I'm paying a visit to the Millers tomorrow. I don't want you talking to Beanpole. If you see him, just keep away, *ja*?"

"I don't want anything to do with Beanpole," Susie agreed, knowing it was sensible. Still, she couldn't bring herself to promise. If Beanpole had something to do with Salome's disappearance, then someone had to bring his sins into the light.

MISSING

CHAPTER FOUR

>> Five Years Ago

Salome Beiler glanced over an armload of clothing at the clock on Mrs. Ashton's wall. She had ten minutes before she was supposed to call and check in on where the guys were. It was enough time to put the clothes in the washer and touch herself up before she used Mrs. Ashton's phone to call Mike on his cell. She'd met Mike three weeks ago. He and his friends were freshmen in college, and the stories they'd told of their lives on campus had made Salome green with envy.

Salome knew it would be difficult for her just to catch up to the *Englischers* in her education, even though she loved reading and had worked her way through a lot of the local library, but she had a plan. Her job allowed her to save money, and when she got enough, she would rent a room in the city. She could work in the daytime and earn her GED at night. But that didn't mean that while she was saving that she couldn't have a *little* fun—and maybe a boyfriend. Not a guy she had to marry, just a boy that she could watch *Englisch* television shows with and maybe kiss sometimes.

Salome sorted Mrs. Ashton's clothing, as always, putting the hang-dry, bright colors, and whites into separate piles. She always washed the hang-dry clothing first so that it could get the most of the warm sunshine on the line. Then came the unmentionables and finally the colors, both of which went into the dryer. When she had her own dryer, she wouldn't bother with hanging another thing, Salome promised herself. One day, she was going to be a lawyer, like the sharply dressed blonde woman on TV who put child abusers in jail.

Salome rubbed at a bruise on her shoulder. She wished a fancy *Englisch* lawyer would come to her house sometimes and take her dad away, but only when he was drinking.

Salome glanced at the clock. It was time. She reached between the washer and dryer and grabbed a bag of *Englisch* clothes. She wouldn't have time to change, but she could at least put on a touch of makeup and pull some dark strands out of their bun to frame her face. Besides, Mike said he liked her Amish clothes because they made her look innocent.

Salome wasn't sure she liked that, but *Englisch* guys were different. And anyway, Mike was sweet. Not at all like the guy in that vampire book she'd gotten out of the library.

She finished with her hair and makeup in the hallway mirror

and then made her way to the kitchen. He'd written his number on the back of a receipt, which she kept in her secret journal under the floorboards behind the barn, but she'd memorized it weeks ago. She slowly dialed the numbers and held the phone up to her ear.

On the third ring, Mike picked up. He was laughing, and so was everyone else, so Salome could barely hear when he said hello.

Salome smiled, careful to keep her voice pitched low. "Where are you guys?"

"Hold on." There was a muffled exchange. "About five minutes away according to Google maps."

"Okay, I'll meet you outside."

"Are you wearing your bonnet?"

"*Ja.*" Salome was annoyed at the question for a second, but she pushed the emotion down. It was good if Mike liked that she was Amish. She just hoped he didn't think she was going to wear boring, plain clothes when she got her own place.

Salome was careful to cinch her apron extra tight before stepping outside, so it at least looked like she had some kind of waistline. She'd spend a little time with Mike and the guys while the clothes were washing. Then she'd be back and have Mrs. Ashton's tea ready before she woke from her nap.

With a light heart, Salome closed the door as softly as she

could behind her and dashed down the circular driveway to the road.

>> Present Day

Jumbo Miller rose, feeling apprehensive. He knew exactly why he felt as he did—it was the fifth anniversary of Salome Beiler's disappearance—her running off. He knew what his son and wife would do today. Beanpole would withdraw even more from everyone, and then he would disappear for several hours. By the time he came back, it would be dark and his coat would be filthy.

Not today. I will keep him busy from dawn to dusk. He will participate with us in reading the Bible tonight.

Jumbo thought of Emma, his wife, and he felt sad and at a loss. He remembered back to their courting days. She had always been spirited and just a little bit different. In those early days of their relationship, he had figured that he would be able to help her get her emotions and reactions under control.

Jumbo shook his head with a sigh. I sinned, thinking that I could exert more control over her than God could. And now, I'm paying for that conceit.

He had long since fallen out of love with Emma, but because of their Ordnung, he didn't try to leave her. In accordance with their rules, he never raised a hand to his wife, even when she came after him, swinging with her fists and fingernails.

Remembering her attack of just a few days ago, Jumbo rubbed a big hand over his cheek. Thankfully, the bruise was beginning to fade.

If only he'd had the strength to keep to the Ordnung in all things. But wasn't it his duty to see to the health and wellbeing of his family? As unstable as his wife and son were, the last thing they needed were outsiders tromping around their lives, asking questions.

Besides, he'd seen Salome just a week prior to her disappearance, standing by the side of the road in *Englisch* clothes, chatting with a station wagon full of *Englisch* boys. She'd leaned in the window and kissed one of them on the lips!

Salome had run off with them for sure. She'd talked since she was a girl about leaving the community for her *rumspringa*. She'd been troubled and unhappy in the community. Of course she'd run off!

End of the story.

If Jumbo hadn't actually *seen* Salome getting into the station wagon that day as he'd said...well, he'd seen enough before. He had no reason to suspect anything else. So why did he still feel this oppressive guilt? Just because Beanpole had wanted to court with Salome didn't mean her running off had anything to do with Jumbo or his family. His son was strange, but not violent, at least not violent like Emma.

And yet, this anniversary sat uneasy with Jumbo. His son's

reaction—or lack of it—to Salome's leaving had been odd. Today, especially, he hated to let his son out of his sight.

Going downstairs to the kitchen, he told Emma. "I'll be in the barn feeding the animals. Where's Andrew?"

"Beanpole? That useless wretch? I don't know. He wasn't in his room when I came downstairs." Emma slammed the cover on the pot of oatmeal bubbling on the stove.

Jumbo sighed and went outside. In the barn, he saw that the horses were all there, which meant that Andrew had decided to walk.

There was nothing wrong with taking a walk. Fresh air was good for the mind and soul. Still, Jumbo couldn't shake the sense that something was wrong.

I should have gotten up even earlier so I could catch him before he disappeared.

MISSING

CHAPTER FIVE

>> Six Years Ago

The *Englisch* cottage that neighbored Jumbo Miller's farm had long since gone to pasture. Its owner, an elderly widow who had passed on nearly a quarter century ago, had left the house to her son, who had in turn locked the doors, moved to California and left the place to rot. But the tiny two-story cottage had been vibrant once, and its foundation was sturdy still, though the red paint on the outside walls was faded and peeled, the glass of the second floor window had cracked, and shingles were missing from the roof.

Five chipped stone steps led up on a slant to the front door, and an array of rusted tools leaned on the wall beside it. If there'd been a railing, it had been missing for as long as Beanpole had been coming there to hide out from his *mamm*'s moods and his *daed*'s silences. For Beanpole Miller, the tiny farmhouse was a haven…a heaven. As a child, when the other boys had found his odd ways too difficult to ignore, he'd come here and played with his imaginary friends. For them, he was the King.

When Beanpole was eleven, one of the voices had led him through the overgrown garden to a handle sticking straight up from the ground. Pulling up with all of his might, he'd managed after three tries to pry it open. A rush of damp, musty air had washed over him. Taking up a fallen branch from the ground beside the house, he'd walked down a rusted metal ladder into the basement. From there, it had been easy to get into the house and make it his own.

It had been a sign from God when the widow's son had put an ad in the Amish paper for a maintenance man, and Beanpole had taken the job.

Beanpole knew that God meant for him to marry and raise his kinner in this place. And now, at nineteen, it was past time for him to bring his wife home. He stood in the kitchen, resting his hand on the dusty counter, as flashes of his future with Salome flashed through his mind. The stove was no longer stained with rust, but instead was gleaming white. Salome was singing softly in her dusky alto while she stirred at a bubbling pot.

"Beanpole, you're home," she said, looking up with a bright smile. Unlike his *mamm*, Salome never shouted after him that he was useless or a wretch. She never flicked ladles of boiling water at him because he'd gotten underfoot. Instead, she looked on him with serene and steady eyes like an angel. Her belly had begun to grow round. Beanpole crossed the room, and pulling her away from her work, he wrapped his arms around her. Desire stirred as he imagined holding her and feeling the heat of her lips against his.

A frantic scraping from the second floor pushed Beanpole from his fantasy. Squirrels had gotten into the attic again.

Guilt washed over him. "I'm sorry, my love," he muttered with tears burning at his eyes. "I'll have it perfect for you. I promise."

Still muttering promises to his beloved, Beanpole took the broom from where he'd found it in the bedroom closet years ago, and went upstairs to take care of the squirrels.

It had to be perfect. Nothing but the best for the woman he loved.

>>Present Day

Susie was grateful that men and women were kept strictly separate from each other at the church service because it meant she could avoid crossing paths with Beanpole Miller. But she hadn't given up on her investigation.

Joe had said that Beanpole had mentioned courting with a girl from Ephrata. Mary Graber, Mark Graber's wife, had come from Ephrata. They'd met on their *rumspringa* when Mark had apprenticed in her district. Susie made it her mission to get a few moments with Mary before the end of the day. Thoughts of how she'd bring up the subject occupied her mind through the whole service. If asked, Susie knew she'd have no idea what the sermon had been about.

The weather was fair so after the service the men lifted the long benches and carried them out of the Stoltzfus barn and onto a grassy patch beneath the shade of a large willow. It had rained just before dawn, cutting some of the humidity, and the grass glistened with the memory of the morning's squall. Susie and the other younger women went to the kitchen to help bring out the meal. The older men would eat first, after which the older women, and then the children of both genders. Because they were outside, the fellowship was more of a picnic style with worshippers taking plates and spooning out what they liked before finding a bench, or more likely a patch of grass, to sit down and relax with friends.

Susie spotted Mary almost immediately. She was sitting with some of the other young mothers on a blanket with a pair of toddlers running and tumbling on the grass around her.

Susie made her way over to the blanket with her plate. When she got close enough, the other three women looked up, one smiling with a wave. That was Maisie Graber, well known for her sunny disposition and incredible baking skills. Susie smiled and sat down on the edge of the blanket beside Mary.

"Oh! Your little one is coming along quite nicely," Maisie said with a laugh. "Is the baby kicking yet?"

Susie grinned. "Like she wants to start her own dance troop."

"*Ja*, John was the same. Maybe you are going to have a little boy." She waved a languid hand over toward the toddlers, one blond haired with a dusting of freckles over his round cheeks.

"Oh no!" Mary cut in. "It's the girls the kick the worst."

That started a good-natured argument about the nature of babies. They made small talk, eating their food in the pleasant sunshine. Susie wanted to talk to Mary alone, and she got her opportunity when they were finished eating. Mary held her hand out and said, "I'll take the plates back to the kitchen if you keep an eye on David." Susie, recognizing her opportunity, also stood. I'll help."

They gathered up the plates and, side-by-side, walked together across the field and driveway back to the farmhouse. The farmhouse was large, which made sense for a family of nine, and they had a porch on the front and back entrance. The door at the back porch offered direct access to the kitchen. When Susie felt that they had gotten far enough away from the other women to speak without being overheard, she looked over at Mary and asked, "I haven't had as much time as I'd like to talk with you. You're from Ephrata right?"

"Yes, I am."

"I don't know… Do you know Beanpole?"

"I don't want anything to do with Beanpole."

"So you…? Did he court with somebody in your district? I heard that he had."

"That wasn't a courting." She leaned closer and slowed her steps. "I know it's a sin to gossip, but…"

It *was* a sin to gossip, but something was clearly weighing on Mary's heart, and it would only take gentle encouragement to get her to talk. If it meant finding out what had happened to Salome, then that seemed a small price to pay.

Susie said, "It's not gossip. I'm just a bit worried about a friend." That wasn't exactly a lie.

That was that Mary needed. It was like the flood gates opened. "I wasn't there. But it happened to Fannie—Fannie Graber, now Melcher. She was my sister's friend. She was coming home from one of the Sings, and one of the wheels on her buggy had trouble. She had to pull over.

"It was after dark in late July, and Fannie was all by herself. She hopped out of the buggy to take a look at the wheel. She had planned just to wait for somebody to come along to help when she saw Beanpole. He was driving his buggy and when he saw her, he pulled over.

"At first, Fanny said she was relieved, but then Beanpole began acting strangely. He walked over to her and knelt beside the buggy to look at the wheel, which seemed normal enough, but then he grabbed her hand. He started telling her how much he admired her, and he then began to ramble something about how he had been wrong the first time, but now he knew God had made his match."

"That was in July?"

"Yes. He had just started coming to our district events. I don't know why or what made him come so far. He said that he was thinking of apprenticing with our carpenter, old Mister Stoltzfus, but he really only came to the Sings and once to a volleyball game."

"What happened to Fannie?"

"He grabbed her by the wrist, and she asked him to let her go. He shouted at her, and then she shouted back at him. Fannie wasn't the type to let someone intimidate her. She still isn't. But then it went beyond words, and he started to drag her to the buggy. So she did this thing that her brother had taught her from some martial arts class he was taking on his *rumspringa*. Aikido? I don't know. All I know is that she yanked her wrist somehow and when he let go, she ran. He chased her, and she said she had never been so scared, but then some of the other youths came rattling down that tiny back road.

"They must have left later or took a different route, I don't know. She called out to them. And Beanpole ran off. Later, she reported to the Bishop and to her family. Beanpole was banned from our youth groups, but it didn't matter because he never came back. I don't know how much of it was him just being off, or if he would have done her any harm, but I never much liked Beanpole after that. He scared me. But since Fannie just wanted to forget about it, and Beanpole has never really done anything to me, I had to let it go.

"I did speak to John's mother about it though. She said that it was better not to wake up the sleeping dog and that my husband and I should go about our lives and stay away from Beanpole. So that's what I've done."

Susie took Mary's hands. The other woman was shaking. She shook her head. "I'm sorry. I shouldn't have said so much."

"No. I'm glad you did." The more Susie learned about Beanpole, the more convinced she became that he had had something to do with Salome's disappearance. Her insides felt cold as she thought about it. If Beanpole had done something, then where was Salome now? She couldn't believe that he had done something irrevocable. Salome had to be alive. And yet, wherever Salome was now, Susie had no choice but to face how horribly she had failed her best friend.

She wasn't going to fail Salome again. This conversation with Mary only made her more determined to learn the truth of things. One way or the other, she would find the reasons behind Salome's disappearance and bring them into the light.

MISSING

RUTH PRICE & SARAH CARMICHAEL

CHAPTER SIX

>> Five Years Ago

There went Beanpole again, sidling up to that no good trash Salome. He handed her a plate of what looked like applesauce cake. Salome smiled, and like a flower to the sun, Beanpole leaned toward her.

Disgusting.

It was as if none of them had listened to the sermon. For too many of the young people, Church was all daydreaming, singing and socializing. They couldn't hear the whisper of God in their ears.

Emma heard it, and she listened.

When the Lord had told her to drown that litter of kittens in the barn, she'd done it, no matter how Beanpole had cried as he tried to wrench the little wretches from her hands. And then there was her second daughter, Annie. She'd had the mark of the devil on her forehead—a wine colored tear, plain as day. Listening to the Lord that night had been hard. She'd begged Him for another test, but He'd put her palm to the pan for resisting, and so she'd done what had to be done. She still had the scar on her hand. It was a fair punishment for trying to make her own way.

Even though she knew she'd done right, that night still haunted her. The infant had struggled; her pitiful twitches under the baby pillow almost making Emma lose her resolve.

But Emma was strong. She heard the Lord and listened, and the Lord didn't like Salome.

What do I do, Gott?

The Lord was silent.

No. Not silent. There was just too much commotion out here, with the food and fellowship. It drowned out the Lord's Word. Or maybe her husband had mixed those pills into her coffee again.

Ja, maybe. He'd gone to town on Thursday.

No matter. No food or drink would cross her lips until she got an answer. Reluctantly, she walked her plate of food back to the kitchen. The smothered chicken was making her mouth water. But the needs of the soul were stronger than those of the flesh.

No one was going to take her youngest away from her.

>> Present Day

Andrew "Beanpole" Miller sat alone with his back leaned against the Stoltzfus family's old willow tree behind the barn. Did he always eat by himself? Joe didn't know. He'd never sought out Beanpole to talk before.

As he approached, Beanpole looked up.

"Grasshopper!" he exclaimed with a wave and a smile.

Joe gave a start at his old nickname. Nobody had called him Grasshopper since he was a child.

"Hey, Beanpole. Mind if I sit?"

Beanpole shrugged.

They ate in silence for a minute or so before Joe, realizing that the onus was on him to keep the conversation going, asked, "How's your *mamm*?"

"Same as usual."

"And your *daed*?"

"*Ja*."

This was illuminating. When Joe had said he'd talk to Beanpole and find out what had happened, he hadn't really thought through what he'd ask. 'Hey Beanpole, did you sneak onto my property last week and open up the barn door so the horse could get out?'

That wasn't a casual question. And the follow up, 'Do you have any idea what happened to Salome?' was even less casual.

Beanpole lifted up a cob of corn and started eating it methodically from left to right. When he'd gotten to the end of the first row and swallowed, Joe said, "My wife saw you last week in town. Said you were buying some ribbons, red ones..."

"*Ja.*"

"Is your *mamm* working on a new quilt?"

Beanpole shrugged again.

Joe could see why no one sought out Beanpole for conversation or company. Still, being lousy at talking didn't mean he'd done anything wrong. "My Susie told me her best friend loved red ribbons. You know...Salome."

Beanpole's grip on his corn tightened at the name. "What about Salome?"

"Susie's really worried that something might have happened to her."

"Nothing happened to her."

"Well, she did run off with those *Englischers*. Something might have happened to her with them."

"*Ja.* Maybe."

"So, umm..." Talking to Beanpole was like milking a stone, except less exciting. "When's the last time you saw Salome?"

Beanpole looked up, his eyes shining. "She was an angel."

The rapturous look on Beanpole's face made Joseph's stomach run cold. "When was she an angel?" he asked, speaking slowly and carefully.

"When she sang... Do you remember how Salome would sing?"

Yes, Salome had had a lovely voice. Not that it mattered to Joseph. He'd only had eyes for Susie. Still, to see such obvious worship in Beanpole's face was disturbing. "It must have been tough for you. Did you ever court with anyone else?"

"I promised. I am faithful to Salome."

"Even after she ran off?"

"Those *Englischers* didn't treat her right."

"What do you mean? Did you see them do something to her?"

"I made a promise."

A cold feeling settled in Joseph's stomach. "Okay...but, you didn't see her on the day she ran off?"

Beanpole's eyes narrowed as his gaze focused on Joseph. "Why are you asking about Salome?"

"Susie's worried, that's all."

"Susie needs to keep to her own affairs and out of mine."

"You haven't been by our house recently, have you?"

"Why would you ask that?"

"It's just, Susie's been out sometimes, and we'd hate to have missed you if you came calling."

"Susie should be more careful. She's carrying a *bobbeli*, isn't she?"

Joseph started. It wasn't a defiance of the Ordnung to talk so baldly about another man's wife, but that didn't make it polite either. "Susie's doing just fine."

"*Gutt*, I'm glad." He took a bite of his coleslaw.

Joseph doubted he'd get any more from Beanpole today. So he went back to eating. When he'd cleaned his plate, he stood. "Well, I'm glad we had the chance to talk, Beanpole." It wasn't a lie. He was glad he'd talked to the man. If nothing else because, no matter what might have happened five years ago, Joseph was convinced he didn't want Beanpole anywhere near his wife now.

The other man nodded. "Thanks for stopping by," he said with a smile. "Most everyone avoids me."

Joseph's face heated. "Who told you that?" Now he felt guilty. The only reason he was talking to Beanpole was to appease his wife.

"Nobody had to tell me," Beanpole shrugged. "Just is, that's all."

"Well…" Joseph couldn't reassure the man without lying to him, which he would not do. "You take care of yourself, Beanpole."

Beanpole nodded, and then focused his gaze on the plate on his lap. "Mmmhmm."

CHAPTER SEVEN

>> **Eight Years Ago**

"Beanpole!"

"Coming, *Mamm*!" He ran into the kitchen. "I got the potatoes out of the garden like you asked."

"*Gutt, gutt.*" His *mamm* was smiling. Studying her face from a distance, Beanpole relaxed a bit. This was a kind smile, not the mean one. The smile that meant she'd let him lick the spoon on the cakes and pat him on the head and tell him how God had chosen them both specially to carry out His will. Beanpole edged closer. In his arms, he held a sack of potatoes. "Put them on the counter," *Mamm* said. "And help me chopping the vegetables for this stew."

Beanpole did as he was told. When he did as he was told, it made God happy, and that meant *Mamm* didn't smack his fingers with the spoon.

Daed was out in the fields, doing important work with Crabapple John, Beanpole's next oldest brother. Beanpole had wanted to help too, but with no sisters in the house, someone had to stay with *Mamm* and keep her from doing unseemly things, like drowning another litter of barn kittens.

When *Mamm* was kind though, these afternoons were nice—special. He walked to the sink and started washing the dirt off the potatoes. He'd put the first one on the dish grate to dry when his *mamm* said, "There's dirt on that one. Get the wire scrubber."

It looked clean to Beanpole, but he knew better than to argue. He looked under the sink for the stainless steel scrubber. The box said it was for pots, but *Mamm* used it for lots of stuff—the stove, counters, and apparently potatoes.

Holding the scrubber in his hand, he began to move it gently over the skin of the potato. In spite of his best efforts though, the heavy wire put scratches in the skin. After a few seconds, Beanpole ran the now scoured potato under the water and put it back to dry.

His *mamm* sniffed at the pot and smiled. She took the wooden ladle and dipped it inside. Holding the spoon to her lips, she blew and tasted the broth. "Mmm." She took another spoonful and held it out to Beanpole. "Try this."

Beanpole tasted it. His *mamm* had added tomatoes to the

beef stock, and it had a rich flavor that made his stomach growl. "*Gutt*," he said with a grin.

"How old are you now, Beanpole?"

"Seventeen, *Mamm*. My birthday was last month."

"I remember your birthday, boy," *Mamm* snapped. "Eighteen hours of agony. You came out in blood, Andrew."

Beanpole swallowed. He didn't want to think about how babies were born. The other boys whispered about it sometimes after Church. The same way they whispered about kissing girls and—*NO!* He wouldn't let his mind go down the path of sin, especially not in front of his *mamm*. She had a way of knowing these things.

"You're getting old enough to start courting, aren't you, Beanpole."

"Not thinking about courting, *Mamm*." Though he was. There was one girl who'd always held his attention. Once he got old enough to court, he was going to ask Salome to marry him.

"*Ach*, boys are always thinking about courting…and what comes after. Having baby after baby doesn't hurt men none."

"I wouldn't hurt her," Beanpole said.

"Who?"

Beanpole laid the second potato next to the first. "Nobody," he mumbled.

"Oh, there's somebody. I can see it in your eyes. I birthed you, Beanpole. You can't hide anything from me."

It was true. *Mamm* had a way of ferreting out his secrets. Like the comic book Samuel Stauffer had given him in the second grade that Beanpole had hidden under his mattress. Beanpole had paid for that one. They'd had to drive all the way to the clinic to get his arm set and put in a cast, and he'd been forbidden to talk to Samuel again. It made him mad to think about what had happened, which was also a sin. In spite of his best efforts, Andrew "Beanpole" Miller knew he was full of sin, and it was only getting worse as he got older.

"I'm sorry, *Mamm*," he said again, but he couldn't bring himself to mean it as he ought to have. Samuel had gotten in trouble then, too. His *daed* had given him a firm talking to, and he was put on the worst chores for a month, but his *mamm* hadn't broken his arm.

"Don't give me that stubborn look, Andrew Miller."

"Sorry."

"I'm just interested to see how my son is growing up." Her hand darted to his head. He flinched, but instead of a blow, she only ruffled his hair gently. "I care about how you're coming up. That you're setting to live a Godly life."

"*Ja, Mamm.*"

"So, how long are you going to keep this a secret? Who is it that turns my sweet baby's face red? Katie Stauffer?"

"*Ne!*"

"Then who is it? I see you looking across the aisle at the Church meetings. It's the way of young people to grow up, start courting, and have families of their own."

Beanpole knew that voice. His *mamm* wasn't going to give up until she got an answer. Better to tell her now, while she was in a good mood, than get found out later when she was in a temper. "Salome Beiler," he mumbled.

"Who?"

He said it again and then backed away as his *mamm*'s eyes widened in horror. "Salome Beiler?! Her *daed* is a drunk!"

"*Ne!* Drinking alcohol is against the Ordnung!"

Mamm shook her head. "You're too young and too stupid to understand. He drinks the fruit of the vine, and it's tainted him—tainted his blood. *Ne*, I won't have you courting with Salome Beiler!"

Beanpole gritted his teeth. He didn't believe his *mamm* about Salome's *daed*. And even if his *mamm* was right, that didn't mean that Salome was bad. She wasn't. He loved Salome. Once, when they were both in the eighth grade, she'd pulled up the sleeves of her dress to run a race against Mary Hoffstetter, and he'd seen the bruise circling her arm, just above her wrist. He knew those kinds of bruises because sometimes his *mamm* grabbed him the same way.

Salome understood. And Beanpole had made himself a promise: when they got married, he'd be the best husband for her. She was perfect, not bad like him, so he'd have no reason to hurt her. He wouldn't drink or be cruel. And in return, she would love him back. She'd love him unconditionally, as God was supposed to.

"I'm going to marry Salome Beiler," Beanpole declared. He looked up at his *mamm* defiantly.

His *mamm*'s eyes narrowed. Before he could react, she had grabbed him by the hair, which was curling just past his ears and in desperate need of a haircut, and pulled.

He screamed.

"Quit whining! Tell me you're not going to court with that no good Salome Beiler."

"I won't!"

"She's bewitched you. I tried so hard to be a good *mamm* to you, and—" His *mamm* sobbed, but her grip stayed tight. "You know what the Bible says about maintaining a pure heart, don't you? Second Timothy 2:22, 'Flee the evil desires of youth, and pursue righteousness, faith, love and peace, along with those who call on the Lord out of a pure heart.' Do you understand what that means?"

"There's nothing wrong with Salome!"

"I won't have you giving way to lustful thoughts."

"I'm not! I won't! I promise."

She twisted his hair one more time, digging her nails into his scalp before finally, blessedly, letting go. "*Gutt.* That one's not clean yet," she said, throwing the first potato back into the sink.

A smear of his blood stained the skin. Beanpole scrubbed.

>> Present Day

"I can't thank you enough for driving me," Susie said as she and her new friend Tiffany zipped down the road in Tiffany's navy blue SUV.

Tiffany laughed. Her hands rested on the steering wheel with the ease of long practice. "Least I can do, Suz," she said. "It's so nice to know someone here. And those sticky buns you made when you had Malcolm and me over for dinner… Malcolm won't stop bugging me to try out your recipe."

Susie smiled. She was grateful for Tiffany's friendship, too. For one, it wasn't as if she could share her suspicions with anyone in her own district. Especially since Joseph had been so forceful after his conversation with Beanpole, wanting Susie to stay out of things. "I know it's stupid. I mean, I'm having a baby, and here I am trying to solve a mystery that isn't even really a mystery."

"The cops should have done more to find your friend."

"Jumbo saw her get into the car with those *Englischers*."

"Isn't he this Beanpole guy's dad?"

"*Ja*."

"Well, he's a bit biased then."

"There's no reason to think Beanpole was involved."

"Yeah, that's why we're driving to this Ephrata district to talk to another woman this Beanpole guy assaulted. You're not stupid, Susie. And your husband thinks something's up too, otherwise he wouldn't be trying to keep you away from this guy. Sure, maybe you're wrong about him and your friend, but there's no harm in finding out for sure."

Susie nodded, and a weight lifted from her shoulders. She wasn't exactly defying her husband, but that didn't mean she was 100% in the right either. And she was glad to have someone else, a person who had no connection to what had happened, believe in her.

Susie shifted in the chair. Her lower back had been aching all morning. The feeling made her nervous, and she rested her palm on her stomach. Back pain was normal for pregnancy as it advanced. At the same time, when she'd lost her last two babies, there'd been pain in her back and stomach. But both had been too young to kick. This baby had been doing the usual tap dance all morning.

Susie took a sip of the bottled orange juice that Tiffany had picked up for both of them this morning as Tiffany turned off the main road onto a narrow road. Her GPS system said, "In 200 yards, turn right. Your destination will be on your right."

Looking out over the cornfields on either side of the road, Tiffany said, "I think you're going to have to take it from here."

"Just pull into the closest driveway and we'll ask for directions to Fanny's house," Susie said with more confidence than she felt.

"Good deal. My phone will take recordings, and I have an app that will get whatever your witness says transcribed, just in case."

Susie was amazed. It hadn't even occurred to her to record the conversation. That sort of thing wasn't a part of her Amish lifestyle, at the same time, in a situation like this, it was definitely useful. "*Danki*," she said, knowing that Tiffany would understand. She'd asked to learn and tried using a few phrases of Pennsylvania Dutch when she and her husband had come for dinner.

"No problem. It's just good to get out of the house. And look at us, two pregnant lady detectives. Who said life stopped with motherhood?"

"Someone says that?" For Susie, it seemed like her life would finally, truly be starting.

Tiffany laughed as she stopped the car in front of a large, white farmhouse. "Okay, you do the talking. I can only say 'good' and 'thank you.'"

The front door to the farmhouse opened, and a woman stepped onto the porch. Susie opened the car door and stepped out. The woman, seeing that Susie was also Amish, greeted her in Pennsylvania Dutch. "Good morning. Are you—? I don't think we've met"

"*Ne*. I'm from Bird-in-Hand. I was hoping you could help me find Fannie Melcher's home."

"Bird-in-Hand..." She breathed sharply through her nose. "We haven't had anyone here from your district in a long time. Is there a problem?"

"No. Mary Graber said she might want to talk to me. It's personal."

"Oh," she nodded. "I see. I hope everything's okay..."

Though gossiping was a sin, and against most every district's Ordnung, Susie didn't miss the other woman's expectant expression, or the way she let the silence linger between them. She wanted to know what had brought Susie to her district, and she was hoping by hook or crook to drag it out of Susie.

Susie said, "Everything's fine. I was just hoping for directions."

"*Ja*, of course." The woman's shoulders slumped in poorly hid disappointment. "Just down that road a bit, turn right at the second grain silo. They're down the driveway, first house."

"*Danki!*" Susie said brightly. Her stomach ached, probably from worry. She rested her hand on her stomach. "It's okay, little one," she whispered in her mind. "We'll be back home before we know it."

Susie got back into the car and gave Tiffany the directions.

"Are you okay, hon," Tiffany asked. "You're looking kind of green."

"Fine," Susie said. "Just nervous, I think. And my back's been giving me trouble."

"I hear ya, sister. Between that and my uterus crowding out my bladder, I'm in and out of the bed all night. I'll be so glad when this little bruiser is finally done cooking!"

Susie laughed. "*Ja*."

As they pulled up into the driveway, Susie had a flash of nervousness. It's not as if she was expected. What if they were out? What if she'd had the wrong name? What if they didn't want to speak with her at all?

Outside, in the pasture, two horses looked up languidly at the car as it stopped.

No, she was doing this for Salome. She wouldn't chicken out now. Her mouth was dry, so she took another swig of the orange juice and then forced a smile. "Guess we'd better knock."

Before she could let the gnawing, aching fear in her gut force her to turn back at the threshold, she opened the passenger-side door and stepped out. The sun had been playing hide and seek with fluffy, white clouds through the entire morning. Now it was out, kissing light over the barn, pasture and cornfield farther off.

Tiffany said, "I think they're out back." She pointed to the side of the house. "Looks like they're hanging out some laundry."

Susie walked towards where her friend was pointing. At that moment, a small child of maybe three years old came dashing toward them from the side of the house with a preteen blonde girl fast on his heels. "John!" the girl shouted.

"Car!" the boy shouted in Pennsylvania Dutch.

The girl grabbed the toddler by the waist and lifted him up. The boy laughed, flailing his arms and legs.

"Stop kicking!" the girl ordered. "I'm sorry," she said, looking up at Susie. "He really needs a nap."

"No nap!"

Susie sighed. In a couple of years, it would be the same for her—hopefully with less screaming.

"It's fine," Susie said, looking down at the boy. "You should mind your sister."

"Cousin," the girl said. "I'm just helping out Aunt Fannie today since she has two kinner, and with all of the laundry…"

"*Gutt*," Susie said with a nod.

The door to the main house opened, and a plump woman stepped out onto the porch. She held a cloth bag filled with clothespins and balanced a baby on her hip. "Katie?" she said.

"They're here to talk to you, Fannie."

"*Mamm!*" the little boy shouted. Tantrum forgotten, he scrambled to his feet and wiped his hands on his trousers. "Car!"

"*Ja*," Fannie said, stepping down off of the porch and walking toward them. She stopped when she reached Katie's side. "My husband's gotten work at the carpentry, so it's just me and Katie and the kids until six."

"I'm sorry if this is a bad time," Susie said.

"*Ne*." Fannie's brow furrowed as she looked from Susie to Tiffany and back again. "Can I help you two with something?"

"My name's Susie Zook and this is my friend Tiffany Jackson. I'm from Bird-in-Hand. Are you Fannie Melcher?"

"*Ja*."

Susie took a breath. "I know it's been a long time, but I was hoping I could talk with you for a few minutes about Andrew

Miller—Beanpole."

The open smile on Fannie's face froze, and she shifted the baby on her hip. "I don't want to have anything to do with him," she said. "You should stay away from him." She looked down at Susie's pregnant belly. "You're not...not with Beanpole—?"

"*Ne!*" The thought filled Susie with horror. "*Ne,* my husband is Joe Zook. But Beanpole had thought he was courting with my best friend, Salome."

"Salome?" Fannie's eyes widened. "He talked about her. He said she took up with some *Englischer.* I think that's—" Fannie turned to Katie and held out the bag of clothespins. "Can you take John to the back and finish hanging the laundry?"

"But—"

"Please, Katie. I need to speak with these ladies privately."

The girl nodded, and taking John by the hand, started to lead him back to where the laundry line was strung in a zig-zag from the house to a large oak tree.

"I'm sorry," Susie said. "It's just..."

"Come in. Can I offer you some tea? When are you due?" She glanced over at Tiffany. "Both of you!"

"Around Christmas," Susie said at the same time Tiffany said, "January. And I'm not married to this Beanpole either. I can keep an eye on that girl and your son if you'd like. Susie asked me for a ride and—"

"No, you shouldn't be standing outside in the elements. We'll be able to see Katie and Johnathon from the kitchen. Come inside, sit down, and I'll get you two some tea." She started walking to the house.

Left without a choice, Susie and Tiffany followed.

Fannie led them into her house, moving them briskly through the entryway, bright with daylight pouring through three large open windows. A hallway ran along the side of the house, with two windows keeping the area from being too dim to pass. Quilt squares had been hung on the walls, adding splashes of blue and green to the dark wood paneling along the inside wall.

When they reached the kitchen, Fannie waved Susie and Tiffany to a narrow dining table with four wooden chairs and a high chair around it. Susie sat down at one. Her back was aching, and just sitting was a pure relief.

"Are you alright?" Tiffany leaned over to Susie and whispered.

Susie nodded.

Fannie placed a glass of sweet iced tea in front of each of them, and then sat down with a glass of her own.

Susie took a sip, ice clinking as she sat it back on the coaster on the table. "Thank you for having us in," she said, finally.

"It's been a long time since Beanpole..."

"I understand. I mentioned my friend, Salome."

"*Ja*, he talked about Salome." Fanny's lips tightened. "He wasn't— I don't mean to gossip."

"I'm not accusing or gossiping," Susie said. "I'm just concerned about my friend. Mary said that Beanpole tried something on you."

"What did she say about it?"

"That your buggy had gotten stuck and he came up to help you, but then became violent..."

Fannie shook her head. "It wasn't— I mean, he scared me. He was raving about your friend Salome and how he'd saved her."

"Saved her from what?"

"One of the *Englischers* she ran off with tried something with her; he didn't say what. He only said he'd been too late to save her. Then he started talking to me as if I were her, calling me Salome and begging to court with me. It was as if he didn't really see me. He grabbed my arm and started trying to pull me away from the buggy, saying he wanted to take me to our home. That's when I broke his grip like my brother showed me. It was a blessing that Jeremiah and Michael came around in their buggy."

Susie nodded. "You think he would have hurt you?"

Fannie sighed, and swirled the ice in her glass. "I don't know. I've prayed on this. And I spoke with the Bishop after. Beanpole was forbidden from attending our youth groups or spending time in our district. I should have felt ashamed for not even wanting to hear his side of it, but...I don't know. He didn't actually do anything to me, or say anything violent, but I had a bad feeling. And after, I thought I felt someone watching me."

"Did you see him?"

"I didn't see anyone. It was just a feeling. I didn't go by myself anywhere for months. Michael was a real rock for me. And we started courting. It just felt natural. And since Beanpole never came around after that, I just...I wanted to forget about it."

Susie understood that. She'd felt the same, seeing him with the red ribbon. And then there was the person who had opened their barn door in the storm. It was wrong to blame Beanpole without evidence, but Susie felt in her gut it had to have been him.

"And he never came back after that?" Tiffany said. "Did you call the cops?"

"*Ne*. The Bishop handled it."

"You should have filed a police report. A person with that kind of obsession can get dangerous," Tiffany explained. "My sister had to deal with the same thing. She played basketball in college, and this 'fan' started sending her letters and then stalking her after games. Shanae finally had to file an order of protection."

"Did it help?" Susie asked.

Tiffany shrugged. "Some. I think her boyfriend had some words with him too.

Susie said, "I haven't seen Salome in five years. Everyone says she ran off with some *Englischer* boy, but she'd have told me if she was going to do something so drastic."

"Beanpole said something about an *Englisch* boy," Fannie said. "If your friend disappeared, it could have been that."

"Do you think it could have been Beanpole?"

Fannie pressed her lips together and breathed out a sigh through her nose. She shook her head. "Maybe. I don't know. He didn't seem like he wanted to hurt me...her, but..."

Susie nodded. She needed to learn more about these *Englisch* boys. Whatever Beanpole had seen—or done—his story lined up with the others. Salome had been seeing an *Englischer* secretly. It hurt Susie to know her best friend had hidden something so important.

"Maybe she did run off..." Susie mused.

"Just like that?" Tiffany said, her tone disbelieving.

"Maybe I didn't know her at all."

"No," Tiffany said. "I don't buy it. You should talk to those cops, the ones who were investigating what happened with Salome. Maybe they can find something about this boy your friend was hanging with. Worse thing that happens, you track your friend down and give her a good smack for causing all of this trouble."

Susie smiled. If that was the worst thing, she'd consider herself very, very blessed.

Dear God, let this be the worst of it. Whatever I did to make Salome think she couldn't trust me, let me find her and fix it.

But the sense of reassurance she expected from her prayer didn't come. She could still feel the slippery plastic covering of Mrs. Ashton's chairs. She was still waiting for her friend to pop back up. And a part of her couldn't see a good outcome, not even if her prayers were answered and Salome had only run off.

But Tiffany was right. Susie had to talk with the police.

They finished their tea and said their goodbyes. As Fannie led Susie and Tiffany back to her car, the ache in Susie's back grew stronger, and a blinding spike of pain speared through her lower abdomen.

Susie stumbled.

Tiffany steadied her, putting a hand on either side of her upper arms as Susie stopped, cupping her belly with her right hand at the point where the pain had blossomed. It was ebbing now, the memory of a flash of light still spotting her vision.

"Are you okay?"

"*Ja,*" Susie said, catching her breath. The baby kicked. Susie breathed out a sigh of relief. Everything was fine. It had to be. "Must have been a cramp," she said.

"Why don't you sit down some more," Fannie said, gesturing toward one of the living room chairs.

"*Ne,*" Susie said. "We should get back. I don't want my husband to worry."

Though Joe hadn't forbidden her from talking with Fannie, Susie doubted he would be pleased to learn that she and Tiffany had begun investigating things further, especially if the stress was putting the baby in danger.

No. It had just been a cramp. Everything was fine.

When they got back into the car, Tiffany asked, "Did you remember the name of the detectives who were looking into your friend's case?"

"Martinez," Susie said. "And Bartholomew I think." She knew. That day was etched into her mind as if the memories had been chipped in stone.

"Okay, I'll give them a call and see if we can't sit down and have a talk with them next week. We're going to find out what happened to your friend."

"If the police couldn't do it, how are we going to do any better?"

"Because we're two fierce lady detectives, Suz. And we're going to be moms, which means we can handle pretty much anything."

Susie laughed. "I'm so glad we met," she said.

Tiffany nodded. "Me too."

CHAPTER EIGHT

>> Five Years Ago

"Come on, you can have a sip," Mike's best friend Jesse leaned toward Salome, holding out a bottle of beer. His breath smelled of alcohol. Salome wanted to throw up.

"*Ne*, no," Salome said.

"Just a taste. It'll help you relax."

"I'm not drinking," Salome said, leaning back and folding her arms. Why had she agreed to come out here? Mike had always been so sweet to her, since he'd seen her walking along the side of the road from her *daed's* farm to deliver a half-dozen eggs to their neighbor, Mrs. Lapp, who was too old to tend chickens on her own anymore.

Mike had gotten a flat tire, and she'd kept him company, fascinated with his easy smile and the way he'd made her laugh and feel like a regular person.

But now she couldn't help but think she'd made a mistake, sitting here in her Amish dress and bonnet while the other boys glanced at her with a mix of curiosity, confusion, and in Jesse's case, lust.

It had to have been at least fifteen minutes since they'd gotten to this party, a backfield affair about five minutes by car from Mrs. Ashton's. It was one of the fields that had been left fallow for the fall, and groups of teens sat on rocks, stools, and the occasional log around the edge of it.

Salome and Mike shared a damp log furred with moss. Her stockings were damp through her shoes.

"Beer?" Dave, another of Mike's friends, sat on a rock next to the cooler and held out a bottle, glistening with condensation.

Mike hesitated, glanced at Salome. "N-no thanks, Dave."

Mike took her hand. Salome smiled. Some of the tension she'd been feeling eased from her muscles. Mike's friends might be jerks, but Mike cared for her. He wasn't like her father, who would pretend to be good and following the Ordnung until the "need to taste" grew so strong he'd down half a bottle of foul-smelling brew and then lash out at all of them, screaming at imagined slights.

Drinking was against the Ordnung, but it didn't matter because *mamm* would never say anything against her husband,

and the Bishop and her *daed* were close.

It was all hypocrisy. But at least Mike cared. He was good.

Salome squeezed his hand.

"So," Dave asked, "how'd you get away in the middle of the day, Salome? You're Salome, right?"

"Yes," Salome said. Of course he'd forgotten them all meeting up in town a few weeks ago, or the picture that Mike had taken on his phone and gotten printed out at the pharmacy. She'd been so happy in her *Englisch* clothes with her *Englisch* boyfriend's arm around her. Now, she felt like a fish out of water. It wasn't just the clothes. The drinking really made her skin crawl. "We've met before, you know."

"Right, yeah!" Dave nodded, averting his face so Salome couldn't see his expression.

"Yeah," Salome repeated, trying to get the intonation just right. When she was with *Englischers*, she did her best to speak as *Englisch* as possible. This was her future. She hadn't told Susie yet about Mike, but her best friend knew that Salome planned to leave as soon as she'd saved enough to afford a place to live.

And, maybe, she'd have Mike too.

"I work in the afternoons," Salome explained. "But I can get away a bit while the washer is running. Mrs. Ashton doesn't notice."

"Skipping work...you're a bad girl," Dave said. He was smiling, and he stared at her a touch too long. Salome was grateful for Mike's calm presence beside her.

Rumspringa was the time for choosing a husband. Of course, *Englischers* didn't look at life like that at her age. Salome had read enough teen-oriented magazines in the library with Susie to know that. Still, she could hope.

"I do everything I'm supposed to," Salome said. Though she knew she was in the wrong. Mrs. Ashton wasn't paying her to sneak out of the house and spend time with drunken *Englischers*.

And how long had she been gone, anyway?

She leaned closer to Mike and whispered, "What time is it?"

"You have five minutes," Mike said, unclasping his hand from hers and putting it around her waist. He ran slow circles on her hip with his thumb. A warm, pleasant shiver ran through her. Maybe they'd kiss again when he dropped her off at Mrs. Ashton's.

"You're so sweet," he whispered to her. A lock of golden blond hair fell on his temple.

Bold, she lifted her chin and kissed his cheek.

"Whoo-hoo!" Jesse shouted, raising his bottle abruptly, causing some of the beer to slosh out over his hand. "Keep running like that, and you'll get to first base with your Amish hottie before Christmas!"

"Shut it," Mike snapped. "Don't listen to him, Salome," he said, holding her closer.

"I'm not."

"Good."

The sound of a car engine behind her cut over their conversation. Another car was pulling up. It wasn't surprising. These "parties" were more like a shifting gathering of people who came and went as they liked.

But then Jesse turned his head to the noise and whistled through his teeth. "Yo, Mike, Amanda."

Mike dropped his arm from where he'd been holding her, but it was too late.

"Mike! What the...? Who's the bi—?"

"Quiet, Amanda!" Mike jumped to his feet. "It's not what you think!"

"What's not?" Salome stood.

A short, dark-haired woman with perfectly manicured pink nails was running at Mike screaming obscenities. "I didn't believe it when Hayden said you were cheating, but—"

"I'm not cheating."

"Cheating?" Each word was like nails being hammered into

the shattering glass sheet of her dreams. "Mike..."

"Jesse, take her back to her job," Mike said. "Mandy, come on. Let me explain."

"Is she your girlfriend?"

"I can't believe you're cheating on me with an Amish girl."

"We agreed to have an open relationship."

"No, we didn't agree to anything. I said *under no circumstances.*"

"What's an open relationship?"

"You said—"

"We were drunk!"

"C'mon girl." Jesse stood, swaying on his feet. "I got this."

"I'm not riding with you," Salome said. "You're drunk."

"I barely had anything!" Salome forced herself to breathe as Mike, the man she'd thought she might love, grabbed Mandy, his actual girlfriend, by the hand and started walking her toward the trees and making excuses:

"She doesn't mean anything to me."

"No! We didn't do anything. Come on, she wouldn't."

"I love you, Mandy!"

Of course he didn't really feel anything for me. Salome touched her cheek. She was crying. How could she be so stupid!

She decided it was better to know. The fact that everyone lied about her *daed's* secret drinking destroyed the family as much as the drinking itself. She wasn't going to let a lie destroy her. No matter how much the truth hurt.

Salome took a breath. She had to get back to Mrs. Ashton's. They'd driven for five minutes to get here. It would take her at least three times that long to walk home, if she could find her way. She'd best get started now.

She turned from the group.

"Salome?"

It was Dave.

"I have to go back," she said.

"I'll walk you. You shouldn't be alone out here."

"I'll be fine."

"Don't be like that. Come on. I can put the address into the GPS."

She didn't know Dave at all, but what did it matter? What did any of it matter?

"Okay," she agreed.

"What's the address?"

She told him, and he punched the letters and numbers into his phone. "Okay, it'll be about twenty minutes," he said. "We've got to go that way on the side road." He pointed to her left.

She followed.

>> Present Day

Once Tiffany set up the appointment with the two detectives, Susie realized that she needed to double check and make sure there wasn't anything in Salome's things that might help with the investigation. It was a long shot, but better to try. Now that Susie knew Salome had been seeing—and possibly courting with—an *Englischer*, she owed it to herself to see if Salome hadn't left any keepsakes of that relationship behind.

Even before Salome had disappeared, Susie hadn't visited the girl's parents very often. More often than not, Salome would visit Susie, staying for dinner and occasionally spending the night where they'd whisper secrets to each other as they slept shoulder to shoulder in Susie's narrow bed.

Salome had slept curled up like a snail. Susie remembered that Salome kicked when startled, but Susie wouldn't have traded those nights, or her friendship, for less bruised shins. Now, as she pulled her buggy up to the home of Salome's parents, she was struck by the peeling, sun-bleached paint of the family barn. The fields were tended, though the pasture was a bit overgrown as the horse stood ankle deep in uncut grass. Susie pulled up in front of the house.

Her back was still hurting her, and she felt unbalanced as she tied her horse to a pole in front of the house. She'd need a bucket of water for Star. There was a pump next to the barn, but no bucket. She'd have to ask someone in the house.

She started up the stairs to the house. The door to the house opened when she stepped onto the porch.

Salome's *mamm*, Deborah, opened the screen door. She was a thin woman with deep lines around her eyes, lips and between her brows. She stood, shoulders hunched slightly, in a dress that seemed too large and her apron tied tightly to compensate, causing the dark blue fabric of her dress to bunch up in awkward wrinkles above the sash.

"Susie," she said, with an eager expression. "Have you heard from—"

"*Ne.*"

"Ah," Salome's *mamm* sighed. "I was hoping...she wouldn't talk to us even if... Is there something I can help you with?" She held the screen door open for Susie, who took it. "You should sit down for a spell, have something to drink. Coffee?"

"*Ne*, the baby."

"*Ja*," Deborah smiled, an expression that lit her dark brown eyes. "Tea then." She beckoned Susie inside.

The house was quiet, and a layer of dust had settled on the molding though the wood of the furniture had been maintained to a modest shine. What struck Susie most was the silence. Where was Salome's younger sister, Beth?

Deborah had Susie sat down at the head of a long dining table.

"I'll get place settings," she said, before leaving the room.

The house was silent, and a musty chill hung in the air. Milky sunlight shone down through a skylight above. Susie shifted in her chair, and the rustling of fabric and creaking of the chair beneath her was startlingly loud. Susie looked down at her hands. Salome's house had never been so quiet. It was dead inside.

A light squeak of a shoe sole on polished wood sounded from the hallway as Deborah returned, holding two glasses of iced tea and a pair of placemats under her bent arm. She dropped the placemats onto the table. Susie leaned over and grabbed one, orienting it so it was facing the right direction in front of her. Then she did the same thing with Deborah's placemat as Deborah handed Susie a glass.

Susie took a sip.

Deborah sat down, cupping her glass in her hands. "It's good to see you, Susie. How far along are you? Has the baby started kicking?"

Susie smiled. "Like a champ."

"Salome was the same way," Deborah's gaze unfocused, and she stared off at something over Susie's shoulder. "She woke me up in the middle of the night sometimes, dancing around."

"I didn't know that."

"Well... I know you two were close, but there are certain things only a *mamm* can know."

Susie rested her palm on her stomach. The baby was still, sleeping for a change. Still, the movement comforted Susie. "I'd be proud if my daughter had Salome's strength," she said.

"So long as she doesn't run off."

"Do you think Salome ran off?"

"What else could have happened? The police came, but they didn't find anything, and Jumbo saw her get into that car with *Englischers*."

"*Ja*, I know."

"I pray every day that wherever she is, she is happy and well. She is my daughter, in spite of it all."

Susie felt guilty for coming here and bringing the pain of Salome's disappearance back to the surface. How would Susie feel if the same thing happened with her child? It would break her heart. The weight of it seemed to have taken its toll on

Deborah. She had a stoop to her frame, like someone constantly bowing beneath an invisible burden.

"I know you love her," Susie said. "Wherever she is, she has to know that too."

"I just wish I'd been a better *mamm* to her," Deborah said.

"It's not your fault."

Deborah shook her head. "I did my best, but it wasn't enough." She held the glass to her lips, wetting them, and then swallowed, blinking rapidly. "If I'd done better, maybe she wouldn't have...and Beth, she's in New York now with some friends, living as *Englischers*. At least she writes though. Salome..." She closed her eyes.

"That's what I came here about," Susie said. "Salome... I was hoping to take a look at some of her things."

"Why?"

"I'm making my baby quilt, and Salome used to make quilts too. She always had an eye for colors and beautiful designs. I was hoping I might use some of her work, the incomplete stuff maybe, for my *bobbeli's* quilt. I know if she were here, she'd want to give the baby something, and I want my baby to have something of Salome."

Deborah blinked again, her lashes wet with tears. She wiped them away with the back of her sleeve. "*Ja, ja.* That's a beautiful sentiment."

"Well," Susie said with false cheer, "When Salome comes back, she'll be able to see a piece of herself with this little one."

A shiver passed over Susie. Why did saying 'when Salome comes back' feel like a lie?

Deborah said, "I've kept most of Salome's things in her bedroom—hers and Beth's. Why don't you take that tea with you while you look through her marriage chest?"

"*Danki*," Susie said.

"It's just good to speak with you, Susie. And to know you have such faith that our Salome will return to us. Sometimes, I feel it's like she died..." Deborah sighed. "But I'd know if my baby died. I'd have to know."

"You can feel her?"

"I've prayed on this, but..." Deborah's fingers wove together on the glass, almost as if she were praying now. "Whatever happened, I know it was His will."

"Don't give up," Susie said. "You can't let yourself fall into despair."

"Salome always had her secrets. Even as a child, she kept her own council. When she was six, she kept a field mouse in her room as a pet for days. She'd made a little nest out of a cigarette box and was feeding it leftovers: bread, cheese, potato salad. I wouldn't have known if Beth hadn't told me."

"What happened?"

"Her *daed* tried to take it, but Salome fought. She bit and kicked and screamed. It was like nothing I'd ever seen. I had to throw a quilt over her and hold her tight, as if I were wrestling a wild animal, but Timothy got the box. He didn't hurt it. Not like he was having one of his spells. He just let the mouse go in the field, but Salome never forgave him or me."

"I'm sorry," Susie said, the words bitter and ashy in her mouth because she and Deborah both knew the truth.

Timothy's 'spells' had been a result of drink—breaking the Ordnung and drinking. Susie wished she'd told her *mamm* when Salome confessed this to her. But Salome had begged her not to say anything, fearing that her *daed* would be shunned, and the rest of them cast out with him. Susie had been too afraid to lose Salome to risk that. So she'd kept her mouth shut. And Salome had abandoned all of them. Susie couldn't help but feel guilty. She pressed her palm to her stomach.

I will never make that mistake with you, she promised the baby inside. *No matter what, I will fight for you, and I won't be selfish.*

Maybe that was why Susie was fighting so hard now to find out where Salome had gone. She had an apology to make. One for staying silent when they were children, and another for accepting that Salome had simply run away as Susie continued with her own life by marrying and preparing to bring her own baby into the world.

Deborah shrugged. "Salome was always odd. She was too

old for her age in some ways, and always angering her *daed*. I think that even then I knew she was going to leave us. I just thought she'd write, if only on the holidays."

Susie took a sip of her iced tea. Condensation blossomed on the glass, making her fingers damp.

"Let me take you upstairs to Salome's room. Her quilting chest is at the foot of her bed. You can spend some time."

"Danki."

"*Ne*. It's no problem."

There was too much she couldn't say—about Salome's *daed* breaking the Ordnung, the bruises she'd seen on her friend as a child, and the guilt Susie now wore like a concrete jacket. The unspoken words choked her. But she had to look through Salome's things, whatever remained of them, because she owed Salome the truth.

Susie stood, her hand still on her glass. "Do you mind if I start now?"

"*Ja, ja*, that's *gutt*." Deborah stood and wiped her palms on her apron. "*Ja*. I'll take you upstairs. Do you remember where her room is? I'll show you."

"*Danki*." Susie picked up the glass and followed Salome's *mamm* from the dining room, up the stairs, making a right at the top and stopping at the room at the end of the hallway. She hesitated for a few seconds in front of it before taking a deep breath and stepping inside.

"Salome's bed is just how she left it, except I made it up for her. She never much bothered, except when I got cross with her." Deborah pointed to the left bed, which had a neatly stitched patchwork quilt across the top. A chest sat at the foot of the bed, with only a couple of feet between that and the window on the opposite wall.

Susie took another gulp of her tea. Then she placed it on the nightstand and walked to the foot of the bed to open up the chest. A rush of scents washed over her: the smell of mothballs, potpourri, and something else that brought back memories of Susie and Salome's childhood together.

Memories flashed before her eyes like a patchwork of unsewn quilt squares: laughing as they played tag together outside the schoolhouse, stomping in the snow as they traded gifts at Second Christmas, looking over borrowed teen magazines by flashlight underneath the covers, standing at the stove, kneading bread on the counter, their hands covered in flour and flour on Salome's nose and smiling face. Almost eighteen years of memories, stopped abruptly, a clear before and after, the wash of scent transporting her back for a beautiful moment to when her best friend had been with her.

Susie closed her eyes and swallowed down a lump in her throat. She rested her hand on the fabric of the half-sewn quilt that was on the top of the chest, the brief flash of colors embedding in her memory so that even with her eyes closed she saw it, saw her past, and saw Salome as she had been.

Once Susie had recovered herself, she stood, and lifted the quilt out of the chest and onto the bed. Below it was a collection of square scraps of fabric. Some had been cut and sewn into diamond shapes while others were simply pinned. Susie took those out too. Below that was a pair of *Englisch* jeans, skinny and dyed tan, with it a red sleeveless shirt with a plunging neckline.

Susie flushed.

When had Salome worn that?

Susie searched the rest of the chest to the bottom but found nothing else of interest. She felt along the bottom of the chest, just to make sure she hadn't missed anything. Nothing. Disheartened, she sat back on the bed.

She opened the top drawer of the nightstand, which was a lustrous cherry wood. Inside was a notepad with stationary, pastel pink with two cartoon teddy bears on the bottom right corner, hugging. The pad was used, with frayed bits of paper left clinging to the glued spine. Susie ran her fingers over the blank paper. Yes, there were depressions where the tip of the pen had dug grooves through to the remaining sheet on the pad.

Salome had always written with a firm hand, often breaking the chalk when she wrote out her sums on the board on her lap in school. Susie ran her fingers over the pad again and placed it on the bed next to the pile of Salome's unfinished quilt work.

She rifled through the rest of the nightstand, walked over the dresser and with a brief, silent apology, looked through that as well. When she'd finished, she took another drink of the iced tea. The ice had mostly melted, leaving a smattering of sad chips floating on the top.

Well, that was it then. She should go. But she couldn't help the feeling that she'd missed something. Salome had always had her secrets. And a set of *Englisch* clothes wasn't enough. Where were her comic books and magazines? Even if she'd run off, she'd have stored them somewhere.

Susie stood, lifted the quilt and peered under the bed. A small throw rug, like a bathroom mat, was the only thing underneath.

A tingle of excitement ran through Susie. Why would Salome keep a bathmat under her bed? Susie leaned forward on her knees and pulled it out. Then she felt along the floor at the floorboards. Her fingers tingled, and for a moment it felt almost like someone had put their hands on her shoulders, pushing her forward as she tapped at the floor until a hollow echo came back.

Susie pushed at the board and it wiggled under her hand. It was loose! She pressed down hard on one side, and the other came up. Pulling the board away, she peered into the murky darkness at what was, yes, a secret area beneath. Two more floorboards behind the one she had lifted also came up, revealing a plastic bag.

It was a white, drawstring kitchen bag, folded over and tied loosely with one knot at the end. Susie glanced behind her at the door, suddenly fearful of being discovered, before pulling the bag out.

She sat cross-legged on the floor, her round belly jutting out a bit awkwardly as she put the bag on her lap. Her back ached, but she couldn't wait to see what Salome had hidden. Maybe some hint as to where she'd gone?

Carefully, she untied the knot and opened the bag. Inside were two magazines, a makeup compact and tube of lipstick, and a battery-powered flashlight. Susie took everything out and laid it carefully on the floor in front of her.

They were of *Englisch* fashion, one with a dark brown woman on the cover, her head shaved, and the serious expression on her face at odds with the collar of her bright print dress and the sunshine-yellow flower on the headband she wore. Susie flipped through the first magazine, which still smelled faintly of perfume. She could easily imagine Salome admiring the pictures and clothing of the women inside.

A gentle knock sounded against the bedroom door. "Susie, are you okay?"

"*Ja*," Susie said, gathering the magazines back together and pushing them back into the bag. As she did, something fell out, a photo.

Susie was shocked to see Salome grinning out from it. She

wore the same jeans and red shirt that she'd stored in the chest, with her brown waves of hair hanging down, framing her heart-shaped face as she leaned into the embrace of a blond boy with bright green eyes. Two other boys stood on either side of the couple: one stocky and serious-faced wearing jeans and a t-shirt with a logo on it that Susie didn't recognize, the other holding a can of —was that beer?—with his tongue out to the camera.

"Did you need me to take your tea?" Deborah asked as she pushed the door inward.

"Not yet." Susie shoved the bag under the bed. She took the photo and pushed it into the pocket of her apron, neatly tied just above her rounded midsection, just as Deborah stepped inside. Deborah froze, her expression horrified as Susie struggled to stand.

"Susie, why are you on the floor! The baby, you don't want to hurt… I—"

Susie forced a smile. "I'm fine," she explained. "I just dropped something. I got it." She picked up a couple of unfinished quilt squares at random, putting them on her lap as she sat down on the bed.

As soon as the lie passed her lips, Susie felt suddenly guilty. She'd come here on false pretenses, and now she was lying. Still, as terrible as she felt about her sifting through Salome's secrets, she didn't want to expose them further. Not when Salome had had such a troubled relationship with her parents.

"Let me help you clean this up," Deborah said, starting toward the chest. "It's *gutt* to see you here. *Gutt* that you're doing so well. I do hope you'll bring the baby around, when you've had a chance to get yourself recovered from the birth, of course.

Deborah bustled around the bed, smoothing the quilt around Susie as she sorted through the remnants of Salome's work. She placed things in neat piles, the unpinned fabric sections, the pinned ones, the half-sewn section that had been almost finished. When she got to the *Englisch* clothing, she stopped and sat with her head bowed.

Deborah swallowed and clutched one of the pants legs in her hands. "She didn't tell you anything, did she?"

"*Ne,*" Susie said. The hidden photograph was a heavy weight on her conscience. She should say something about it. Deborah deserved to know. But Salome had pried up the floorboards and stored her secrets for a reason, and Susie didn't feel right about exposing them until she knew the truth. Until she knew what it was that she was sharing. She owed Salome that. And if she did track Salome down, it would be better for Salome to decide for herself what she wanted known.

Deborah shook her head. "I'm just glad to have someone here. I always prayed I'd have grandchildren—lots of them. Now with Salome run off and Beth gone, and Michael in Ephrata with his new wife's family... I know I should be grateful for all I have, but..."

Susie put her hand on Deborah's shoulder. "I'm sorry."

Deborah took a deep breath and swallowed again. "Me too. Could you... I mean if for any reason Salome gets in contact with you, can you just let her know I miss her?"

"Of course. How's your husband doing?"

"My husband? *Ja*, of course, he misses her. I mean—"

"Does he still drink?"

Deborah froze, and Susie felt like the worst kind of monster. At the same time, turning a blind eye on the truth was what had led to Salome hiding herself from everyone. "How do you—? Salome told you, didn't she?"

"*Ja*, before she left, when we were children. She begged me not to tell anyone though and..." Susie sighed. "Maybe if I—"

"*Ne*, it's not your fault. And my husband is getting help. First Salome, and then after Beth left, he hasn't touched a drop. We've prayed, and he's in a group, like a support group."

Susie was shocked. "He really stopped?"

"It was hard. He'd always hated it, how it made him treat us, but he'd felt like he had to have it. Then Salome ran off, and he and I had a fight. I said I was going to take Beth and go back to Ephrata and live with my *mamm* and *daed* if he didn't stop, once and for all."

"Salome hasn't contacted me," Susie said. "I came here

hoping I'd find something that would let me know where she might have gone."

Deborah lifted her head and looked at Susie, her eyes shining. "Did you find anything?"

"Maybe. I was hoping you'd let me take some of her things with me—more than the quilts."

"Take what you want, if it helps. Whatever you want."

"*Danki*." Susie sighed. "If I find out anything, I'll let you know. I promise."

Deborah's eyes were shining as she stood. "Let me get all of these things back into the box." She glanced at the quilt squares that Susie had chosen and gave her a stiff smile. "Those are lovely! Blue and green, they will be just lovely." She swallowed. "Salome...she'll be glad to see it when she—"

Deborah gave a choked sob. She knelt down in front of the chest and put her armful of quilt pieces inside. The lid of the chest hid her face from Susie's view.

She doesn't think she'll see Salome again, Susie realized.

And Susie couldn't help the feeling in her chest, like a cold, heavy stone, that Deborah was right, and Susie would never see her best friend again either.

CHAPTER NINE

>> Three Years Ago

After a night of blood, pain, and agonizing loss, Susie had to wait until her husband returned that afternoon to tell him, "We lost the baby." Her voice was flat. She felt numb, like a person riding inside her own body, looking through her eyes, and yet apart—dead.

"Lost, b-but—" Joe stuttered, blinking tears from his eyes. "How? Yesterday…at my sister's…you were fine. You said… Are you sure? We can see the midwife."

Susie shook her head. "It won't help."

"Dear *Gott*!" Joe threw his arms around Susie. It was only when she felt the warmth of him that the grief swept over her, cracking the icy numbness that had held her, like a shield, through the night.

She almost hated him for it. With the warmth of her husband's arms melting her defenses, she had to live again.

"I'm so sorry," Joe breathed into her hair. "I should have been here."

"This was Gott's will," Susie said. The words didn't comfort her. But maybe they would in time.

"I won't leave you again," Joe said.

"We have to bury her," Susie said. "Or him." Her voice cracked. "There wasn't… But I saved… We should bury our *bobbeli* by the tree next to the barn."

"Do you want to talk to your *mamm*? I can go to her home."

"She didn't know. I wasn't going to tell anyone until after three months. No need to burden her now."

"But—"

"*Ne*," Susie said. Her *mamm* was been so eager for grandchildren. The last thing Susie wanted to do was burden her with Susie's failure.

Maybe if Salome hadn't run off, Susie would have confessed to her.

Susie's eyes teared up. She missed Salome. It was worse than her wedding to Joe. Her baby was gone, and instead of thinking about her *mamm* or appreciating the love of her husband, she was reaching out for a friend who had abandoned her without a word.

How selfish was that?

>> Present Day

It was another week before Tiffany could get an interview with Detective Martinez, who was still in charge of the case.

Susie debated telling her husband about her visit with Fannie Melcher, but in the end, like the photo, she kept it to herself. She and Tiffany had done some shopping in town for spices. It wasn't lying to keep details about the rest of the trip to herself. It would just worry Joe to know that she was still sticking her nose into things. And he was already worried enough about Susie and the baby as it was.

Something of her worry must have shone through her attempt at a calm expression, because the day Tiffany was supposed to pick her up to go to the police station, Joe her took in the kitchen by the hands as he was leaving for work and asked, "Are you sure you don't need me to stay home today?"

"*Ne*," Susie said, a bit too quickly. "I'm fine.

"You hardly ate anything this morning. And you've been up at night every day this week. I know you're still worried about Beanpole. I promise, he won't be able to do anything to you. I've spoken with Jumbo. Beanpole won't come anywhere near you. He's been told."

Susie knew that was supposed to be reassuring, and she appreciated her husband's effort, but it wasn't enough to know that Beanpole wouldn't harass her. She needed to know the truth.

"I know you've done everything you can," Susie said. "Don't worry. I'm up at night because this little angel"—she tapped her belly—"keeps kicking me in the bladder at four in the morning."

Joe grinned. "Strong, isn't he?"

"Or she."

"*Ja.*"

"Tiffany is coming this afternoon to take me into town," Susie said. "So don't worry."

"You should stay in. There's nothing we need in town that badly."

"No! I have to—" Susie took a breath and forced a smile. "I'll be fine. It's just better to ride in Tiffany's car than have to maneuver the buggy."

"*Ja*, that's true. Tiffany's a good friend."

"She is," Susie affirmed, feeling a bit guilty. But there wasn't any danger to her in speaking to the police. And the baby was healthy and active, though her back had been throbbing off and on through the last week. But she'd spoken to her *mamm* about it at the Church meeting the past Sunday,

114

and had been reassured that the back pain happened sometimes. There was nothing to worry about.

Maybe she could borrow Tiffany's phone and speak with the doctor without bothering Joe though, who was already under enough stress.

A kicking baby is a healthy baby, Susie reminded herself. And the baby was certainly moving. She needed to calm down and relax.

She kissed Joe goodbye, her expanding belly forcing him to bend down a bit awkwardly to capture her lips, and then watched him on the porch as he drove the buggy down the driveway and out of sight. Then she went back into the house, cleaned up the kitchen, and sat down to do some work on her baby's quilt.

Her baby quilt was almost half finished, with concentric, flower-shaped pieces in the center in pale blue, pink, and green. Laying down the white backing fabric square, she took one of the smaller, light green squares and laid it at the top, right corner, fixing it with a pin. Then she drew a line diagonally through the center. Marking a quarter inch for seam allowance and drawing a second line on the inside, she cut both pieces of fabric and folded it over, pressing it into place.

She did the same thing on the other four corners of the fabric, soon getting lost in her work: measuring, cutting, pressing and sewing as the quilt grew in her hands. The sharp beep of Tiffany's car horn startled her from her work an hour or so later.

She folded the incomplete quilt and set it onto the chair. She stood, grabbed her coat, and stepped out onto the porch. It had rained the night before, and the smell of the fields reassured Susie as she walked down the steps and into Tiffany's car.

"Hey, girl," Tiffany said as Susie buckled her seatbelt. "There's a bottle of water in the cup holder for you."

"Danki."

"No problem." Tiffany yawned. "I was up early this morning with clients—newlyweds, Mennonites. I think they're going to buy."

"That's wonderful!" Susie unscrewed the cap on the water and took a sip. Her stomach lurched. She forced herself to swallow it down, and then put the bottle in the cup holder. She'd been like that all night—nervous. Susie swallowed, trying to get her stomach to settle.

"Are you okay?" Tiffany asked.

"*Gutt*," Susie said. "How's your business going?"

"Great! Super *gutt*! I think I've sold a house. I had such a hard time getting people to listen to me until you and Joe talked me up—"

"I just spoke to a few friends," Susie demurred.

"Thank you so much," Tiffany continued. "Between the

move and the baby, it's been a challenge. Philadelphia was a whole different kettle of fish in the real estate sense, but wherever you are, the hardest part of this business is getting people to know they can trust you."

"Well, I know I can trust you, so all I had to do was spread the word. You can put an ad in the Amish papers, too."

"Don't I have to be Amish?"

"Not at all, I'll put you in touch with Abraham. That said, it's rare for any of us to sell our homes. But it happens sometimes."

Tiffany smiled. "You're good people." Her expression grew more serious. "Are you ready to do this?"

Susie nodded. "I want to help." She had just been glad to learn that Detective Martinez was still at the department and still interested in talking to her about a five-year-old case. "Before, they said there was only so much they could do because she wasn't a minor."

The detectives had taken a police report, but Bartholomew, Martinez's superior, had been clear that an adult couldn't even be declared missing until after 48-hours had passed.

But Martinez had asked a lot of detailed questions. Susie couldn't remember the content of them, she'd been too shaken up, but he'd had kind brown eyes. And he had come back in two days and spoken with the Bishop. With everyone convinced that Salome had run off with *Englischers* though, the investigation had died.

Maybe, like Susie, Martinez believed there was something more to the story too. It seemed so; otherwise, he wouldn't have been so eager, or flexible, about scheduling a meeting with her.

Tiffany kept the conversation light as they drove, soon pulling into the station parking lot. Susie took a final swig of her water before unbuckling her seatbelt and getting out of the car. The station was a line of three squat brick buildings, the main one having a green roof arching to a point like a child's depiction of a standard house. A couple of police officers stood in front of the building, under the awning, as one smoked a cigarette.

They looked up as Tiffany and Susie approached. The smoker, who was thin with a receding hairline, tapped his cigarette on the wall. "Ma'am," he said to each of them, nodding.

"We have an appointment with Detective Martinez," Susie explained.

"He's inside," the smoker said, waving them toward the entrance.

"Thank you," Susie said.

A row of long, wooden benches were lined up back to back down the center of the station lobby. They had backs, and were oiled to a low shine. At the far end of the room was a pair of thick, glass windows. An officer sat behind one.

Susie started to the window. Cool, fluorescent light flickered down on them as they walked. A row of pamphlets was arranged into a hard plastic display that had been screwed tightly to the wall. To the right of the windows was a large metal door.

"Can I help you ladies?" the officer behind the desk said. She was brown, with wide eyes, a narrow face and dark brown hair pulled back into a neat bun.

"We have an appointment with Detective Martinez."

"Yes, hold on." She tapped an intercom button and spoke into it. After about thirty seconds, the large metal door opened. There was a low murmur of conversation and the clicking of people using keyboards. The light scent of sweat, paper, and oil wafted through the open door as Detective Martinez stepped out.

Detective Martinez wore a plaid, button-down shirt, navy suit jacket and matching trousers. He'd gained weight, and he had some lines around his eyes and mouth that Susie didn't remember from before, but his expression was kind and curious. Like before, he made her feel comfortable.

"Thank you," Susie said, "for taking the time to talk with us."

"It's my pleasure. Your friend Missus Jackson said that you had some new information that might be relevant to the case?

Why don't you two come with me to my desk."

He waved them in, and Susie and Tiffany followed him to a bank of desks. In the far corner was a computer. A police officer stood in front of it, typing something.

"Officer Heath is just finishing his reports for his shift," Detective Martinez explained. "My desk is over here." He brought them to a desk with two chairs in front of it. A flat computer screen sat on the right corner of his desk, next to it a cup full of pens, and on the left corner was a metal inbox full of files. Another pair of file folders sat in the middle of his desk. One was open. He sat down, took a pen and a legal pad from under the two files and placed it on top. "Susie Yoder."

"It's Zook now," Susie said, placing her hand instinctually on her belly.

"Oh, congratulations!" His warm brown eyes shone as he smiled at her. "You're looking like six months, is that right?"

"*Ja*," Susie said with a smile.

"Know if it's a boy or a girl?"

"We don't care, as long as the little *bobbeli* is healthy."

Martinez smiled. "Yeah, that's the most important thing. My sister just had a girl. Every day she updates us with a new picture, I mean, online. Well, I know you don't believe in photos, being Amish and all, but it's still wonderful news."

"Thank you." At the detective's mention of photos, Susie

reflexively clenched her finger against her handbag. It was made of simple black leather with a plain clasp.

"So, have you heard anything from your friend?"

He thought that Salome might have contacted her? If only she had! Susie shook her head. "No, I've just... I was hoping you could help me. I know this happened a long time ago, and everyone says she ran off, but—"

"You never believed it."

"I don't. Your partner, Officer Bartholomew, tried to tell me she might have been hiding something, and she was, that's one thing I've learned. She was seeing an *Englischer*, but even so, she wouldn't have run off for years without saying anything."

Martinez's expression grew sharp. "Do you know the name of the boy she was seeing?"

"I think his name was Michael. I found this in her things." Slowly, Susie took out the photo. She'd memorized it by that point. Salome, laughing brightly with a blond *Englischer*'s arm over her shoulder, the pair flanked by two other boys. Seeing her friend again, frozen in time, so happy, made Susie's eyes sting.

Martinez looked down at the photo, his finger resting not on Michael, but the dark-haired boy next to him.

"Do you know him?" Susie asked.

"One minute." Martinez turned on the screen to the

computer and began typing into it rapidly. After a minute, he said, "David Anderson." His expression grew grim. "I'm sorry to have to tell you this, but Mister Anderson was convicted on charges of rape and physically assaulting a nineteen-year-old two years ago. He's currently in prison serving a five-year sentence."

Susie's whole body went cold. The baby, who had been occasionally shifting and fluttering, was still. "He..." Her back ached as another sharp pain ripped through her guts. Susie closed her eyes and tried to breathe.

"Missus Zook, I promise that Mister Anderson can't hurt you. And hopefully he didn't hurt your friend either. It's possible these things have nothing to do with each other. In any case, you've given me new evidence, and that's important."

Tiffany had her arm around Susie's body. "Suz, are you okay? You're looking pale."

"I'm fine." Susie swallowed. The pain was passing again. She'd suspected, possibly, the boy that Salome had been seeing, but this David...she'd barely paid attention to him. "How badly did he hurt the woman he..." she couldn't even say the word. "He hurt."

"I can't go into detail about that—privacy laws."

"Of course."

"This whole case never sat right with me. In truth, I'd thought it might be someone in your community, given how quickly everyone shut down on me. But with this photograph... Do you mind if I hold onto this for evidence?"

"Yes," Susie said. "Yes, of course."

"Thank you so much for your cooperation," Martinez said. "Was there anything else?"

Faced with the thought that Salome had known, and had been friendly with, a convicted criminal—had even perhaps gotten into a car with him—made Susie's suspicions about Beanpole and his red ribbons seem foolish.

Susie shook her head. "I'd been worried that it might have been someone." She shook her head again. Bird-in-Hand was a safe, good community. She was happy and proud to be a member of this district, and to raise her little *bobbeli* in the clean air and sunshine, with a firm grounding in faith and the promise of a bright future. "No, it has to be this guy, David. He had to have done something."

"It's possible. One thing I've learned in this business is that you can't force evidence to fit a theory. It's easy to decide something must be true and then see the facts through your own beliefs. But that's the worst thing you can do as an investigator."

As the detective spoke, Susie felt smaller and smaller. That was exactly what she had done with Beanpole. He'd always been odd. And Salome had loved red ribbons. And then she'd learned about what he'd done to Fannie. But she hadn't even considered that the other boys in the photograph had stories and secrets too.

"You're right," Susie said. "It's really easy to try and make things fit if you get worried or suspicious."

Martinez reached out and put his hand on top of hers. "Thank you for bringing this to me. If you come across anything else that is relevant to the case, please, don't hesitate to contact me."

"And the same if you find out something. How can I reach you?"

Martinez lifted his hand from hers, opened the front drawer of his desk and took out a business card, flipped it over and started writing on it. When he'd finished, he pushed it across the desk to her. "I know you Amish aren't big on telephones, but when you can get to one, you can call me here. That's my number here and my cell. I usually don't give that number out, but this case never sat right with me. Maybe it's because it was one of my first. I always wished I was able to do more."

Susie's eyes stung and her throat felt large and thick. "Thank you," she said again. It was good to hear, and so different from the almost indifferent way Bartholomew had spoken with her before.

She had to accept that sometimes we don't always know the people in our lives as well as we think we do.

Yes, that was true, but it didn't mean that something

couldn't have happened.

"I'll use it," Susie said, taking the business card. Detective Martinez had been attentive and kind, and she was grateful, but the walls of the station felt like they were closing in on her. Two of the other officers were talking, but she couldn't for the life of her understand what they were saying. She felt dizzy and clammy with cold sweat. But the pain had receded. Her back throbbed, but her belly felt fine. She wished she had a glass of water, but there was the bottle in the car.

She stood. The edges of her vision were fuzzy.

That's odd.

It was her last thought before everything went dark.

CHAPTER TEN

>> **Five Years Ago**

On the afternoon Salome Beiler ran off, Jumbo came in from the fields early for a glass of lemonade. It was hot, the kind of hot that dripped sweat into his lashes and made him stop to fan himself with his straw hat every few minutes just to get a hint of breeze. He'd been working, getting the corn fertilized while his son did his regular maintenance job at the old Dietrich farm. Beanpole cared for that falling down farmhouse like it was his own, and while Jumbo didn't like that two afternoons a week all of the home farm work fell on him, he wasn't going to deny his son his independence. Beanpole had precious little of it.

But when he stepped into the kitchen, Beanpole was already back. He leaned over the sink, shoulders hunched. Water hissed into the sink as his son scrubbed at something.

"Beanpole?"

His son didn't move. Only a sharp intake of breath let Jumbo know that his son had heard him at all.

"Son?" Jumbo walked to his son's side. His son gripped a wire scouring pad with his right hand, scrubbing at the left with brutal speed. His hands were raw and bleeding.

Sharp fear cut through Jumbo as he gripped the wrist holding the Brillo pad. "You're clean," he said in his calmest voice. It was exactly what happened when his wife got in one of her moods.

"*Ne*," The boy's hat obscured his face, and his hunched form cast a shadow over the sink. Still, Jumbo couldn't miss the red stains diluting into the water. "I tried to help."

"Can I have this?" Jumbo asked, pulling the bloody scouring pad from his son's hand. Though Beanpole had been working the pad furiously over his skin, his grip on it was weak and Jumbo was able to take it easily. "Now, we should put some bandages on your hands."

Beanpole said, "Salome."

Jumbo's stomach roiled. "What about Salome?"

"That *Englisch* boy was hurting her. I helped! I saved her!" Beanpole sobbed.

"What *Englisch* boy?"

"He never should have touched her."

"Where is he?"

"I saved her."

It had to have been somewhere near the house. But he couldn't leave Beanpole alone, not when he was like this. "Where's Salome?"

"She'll marry me. She loves me. And I saved her."

"That's good…very good. Did she go home?"

Beanpole shook his head.

"Did she say where she was going?"

"She didn't like the house."

"What house?"

"Our house."

Jumbo closed his eyes for a moment as his hopes, his prayers, for his son shattered. Beanpole had inherited whatever it was that troubled his wife. The signs had always been there in the way he sometimes answered questions that nobody had asked, or started projects in the barn that he didn't remember, or his stories about courting with Salome. Even as secretive as Amish youth were when they went about courtships, there was usually some sign, some closeness. But Jumbo had prayed he was wrong. Now, though, he couldn't ignore it. His son had inherited his wife's madness, and that meant that none of them would be free.

"She'll marry me. I'll always be faithful to her. She's my angel."

"What happened to Salome?" Jumbo asked.

"That *Englisch* boy tried to hurt her, but I stopped him."

"Did you hurt him?"

Beanpole looked up, finally, his eyes shining and his lips pulled up in an unnatural grin. "*Ja*," he said. "I hurt him bad—until he left me and Salome alone."

>> Present Day

It was difficult getting away from the house but every Thursday for the past few weeks, Jumbo had a driver bring him into town for his meeting with Larry, an *Englisch* psychiatrist. His wife had been getting more and more erratic, and his son... It was against the Ordnung, but Jumbo knew the others in the district whispered about Beanpole. He'd always been odd and a bit secretive but after Salome ran off, it had gotten worse. There'd been the incident with that girl in the neighboring district—not that Beanpole had done anything—but he had a reputation.

And then there'd been Joe, coming around and asking questions. Could Beanpole have gotten agitated and went out in the middle of the night, causing trouble with Susie and Joe's barn?

On his honor as a Christian, Andrew wanted to say, 'It was impossible that Beanpole had done that,' but the truth was that Beanpole had similar ways to his *mamm*. Ways of being that even with the psychiatrist's help, he was only beginning to understand. Andrew couldn't say he knew his son. And in spite of his best efforts, he wasn't sure he'd done right by his wife or his son either.

Jumbo met Larry at a diner just outside Bird-in-Hand. "Good morning," he said.

"Your cheek... You don't need to tell me if you don't want to, but..."

Jumbo simply nodded, accepting a cup of coffee from the server.

"Was Emma in a mood last night?"

"*Ja,* I detected it almost too late. We were talking about Andrew getting his own place. She wanted him to look in the paper to see if there weren't any widows he might court with, but—" Jumbo shook his head. "I don't feel good about Beanpole leaving. It's natural, I know, but he's always been odd, fanciful, and I don't see him running a farm on his own. I said I'd rather he stays with us and gets a bit more growing up in, even though he is almost twenty-six. And that set her off. She lost her temper and slapped me—hard."

Larry sighed. "Have you ever considered filing police reports, just to get the abuse on the record?"

"*Ne,* she slaps or hits me but in every other way, I am the head of the home."

"I see. Why don't you let me know what you've noticed about her behaviors and moods? This way, even without evaluating her in person, I can give you some possible diagnoses."

Jumbo sighed. "Well, she gets angry very easily. Last night, her words were very slow when she was talking about the unsuitability of the young women for our son. She wants 'only the best' for him. As if I don't!"

Larry wrote quickly. "Okay, anything else?"

"There have been a few times when she...it's hard to explain, but she gets disoriented. And she's said she felt like someone was after her at times. Like someone was looking in through the windows of our house or listening to her words from outside the house. She has always had a hard time getting along with others in Bird-in-Hand, because she feels she is better than they are. More than that, she says she has a special connection with God. But it doesn't seem like prayer. More like she's talking to someone, and they're answering back, and they're not saying good things. I can't explain it."

"What happened the first time she expressed this feeling?" Larry continued listening and writing.

"The deacons and Bishop—our previous Bishop—sat down and talked with her. It was shortly after we married. Our relationship was still wonderful then. They told her that if she didn't publicly repent, she would be shunned, which meant I would also have to shun her. When she heard this, she agreed immediately to repent. She didn't mean it, of course. I found that out just a few years ago. But she made very sure that she didn't communicate her true feelings or thoughts to others since then. She has tried to approach others as though she has the utmost respect for them. But she doesn't." Jumbo pointed at his bruised cheek. "This is what she wants to do to others when she thinks they are being stupid."

Larry continued writing. "Is it the same with Andrew?"

"*Ne—ja*—I don't know. He's never said he heard God talking to him, but he's…" Jumbo shook his head "Sometimes he scrubs his hands until they bleed. And he talks about things that can't have happened. Like how he and Salome Beiler— she ran off five years ago—agreed to get married. He says he's staying faithful to her. But as I said, she ran off with *Englischers*. Mrs. Ashton heard the car. And he does wander off sometimes. He's had a job doing maintenance on Widow Trudy's old property, but he's there every week and stays there too long. And then, Susie Zook said she spotted him in town buying red ribbons. Whatever would he need red ribbons for? I asked him about it and he said he picked them up for someone else, but he wouldn't tell me who."

Larry finished writing and began looking through his scribbled notes. "I'd like to get Emma and Andrew to meet with a psychiatrist to complete a full evaluation. I don't want to make a judgment without seeing them, but I am concerned. It sounds like you and your family need help—therapy and possibly medication."

"*Ne.*"

"There's no shame in it, Andrew."

"I won't have my wife and son on drugs. Already the stigma of having them seen by an *Englischer* psychiatrist is daunting enough."

Larry sighed. "It's their decision what they choose to do, but as I've said before, it sounds like you are having real troubles at home, Andrew. Do you mind just taking a look at something for me?" He reached into his briefcase and took out a file folder. "I photocopied these from the DSM-5."

"What's that?"

"It's a book we use to help us diagnose and assess psychological health concerns." He pushed the file folder across the table. "Without seeing your wife and son, I can't make a diagnosis nor would I want to. But over the course of these conversations we've been having, I have noted some troubling aspects in your descriptions of their behavior. Just take a look over these descriptions and see what you think. I'd like to help, and even if taking medication is off of the table for now, there are things that we can do. If nothing else, if I see them, it will give me a chance to rule out some of the more concerning issues."

That seemed reasonable. Reluctantly, Jumbo took the file folder and pulled it to his side of the table. "Thank you, Doctor."

"Larry, you know I don't hold with too much formality. I've also put my personal cellphone number in that file in case you've misplaced my card. I know you don't hold much with phones, but if you need to, you can call me anytime."

"You know I won't need that, Larry."

"Just promise me you'll read the papers I've given you."

Jumbo would have preferred not to, but Larry had clearly taken a lot of time and effort to put this together, and Jumbo wasn't going to disrespect that effort. "I'll read these," he promised. "All I want is to provide the best for my family. I always thought I'd be a better husband and father."

"If your wife and son are ill, that's not your fault."

Jumbo nodded, but he couldn't quite believe that. "I'll read these."

"Good. And honestly, Jumbo, would you please be careful? Did that slap take you by surprise?"

"*Ja*, she's short and heavy, but she can move fast for all that." Jumbo shook his head. Larry said this wasn't his fault, but as head of the household, it was his responsibility to see to the health of his family. And yet, his second child had died as an infant, and now his wife and son were falling apart. It was good to have someone to talk to. Even prayer could only help so much.

"Are you okay? I know this is a lot take in."

Jumbo sighed. "Emma was always…excitable, but that was a part of her attraction for me," Jumbo confessed. "Back then, she just seemed lively, more than angry or resentful. Only after we had our first two children did things change. I began to notice that her excitability was becoming more…'intense' would be the best word. And soon it became outright anger. I will never forget this. I came home from working in the fields one day. Our oldest child, who is in his thirties now, had a dark bruise on his face. Under his shirtsleeve, he had a cut on his arm. A cut that looked like it had been made with a sharp knife or pair of scissors.

"I asked Emma what happened, and she told me that he had gotten into something he knew good and well was forbidden. Her mood was angry, still. I felt like I didn't want to push things too far with her, but I needed to find out. I went to speak to Robert, and he told me that he had been playing with his little brother rather than picking up their toys and putting them away. That's when his *mamm* came into the living room and took him into her sewing room. There, she told him—and I will never forget what he told me, though I would like to do so— 'If you don't want to help me with your cleaning up, I can always cut off your hand so you can't!' Then, she grabbed her scissors, opened them and cut into the skin above his wrist. Then she slapped him when he screamed out in pain. Those are the cuts I saw.

"I cleaned and bandaged them right away so they wouldn't become infected. I knew I needed to confront her. There's discipline, and then there's abuse. I went back downstairs and, sure enough, she was still really mad. I didn't care. I told her what I had learned, and then I told her she would never again approach our children's disobedience that way. She was to get me or take them to me, whether I was in the house, barn or fields, and let me discipline them. That's when she went after me, just slapping and hitting me everywhere she could reach. There was a knife on the kitchen table, and she grabbed it. This is what she did to me."

Jumbo raised the long sleeve of his shirt, displaying a jagged scar on the inside of his forearm. "It bled and bled, so I had no choice but to take the children with me and go to the emergency room. They treated me and looked at Robert's cut. I managed to get them not to notify children's services by telling them that I had laid the rules down to my wife and that I would be handling their discipline. Something makes me wonder… If I had gone on ahead and let a social worker come out and visit her, would it have made a difference? Would she have gotten as bad as she is now? Other than bruises on the children, she never again went to the extreme of trying to cut off a limb."

Larry shuddered. "Anything could have happened. I'm glad you acted as you did, because it appears that she heard your warning and took it somewhat seriously."

"And then there was Rachel." A memory of the little girl, barely three days old, her little fist touching the wine-colored teardrop birthmark on her temple as she slept peacefully in her bassinet. Jumbo shook his head.

"Rachel, your daughter that passed on as an infant? Do you think Emma had anything to do with that?"

"*Ne!*"

Larry gave him a long, hard look. "What made you think of Rachel now?"

"I'm just upset. Emma had nothing to do with Rachel's death. She wouldn't. She cried for days after."

"I see." Larry nodded. "It's clear all of this is upsetting you. The sooner I can see your wife and son, the better, I think—if only to ease your mind."

"I will read the papers you gave me," Jumbo said. But he made no other promises. As much as he appreciated Larry's professional ear, even these short conversations stirred up too much of his past, too many painful memories.

Better to let sleeping dogs lie, as his *mamm* used to say.

CHAPTER ELEVEN

>> Five Years Ago

Salome and David had been walking for about fifteen minutes when he directed her away from the field that they were skirting and back into the woods. The earth was wet from where it had rained earlier in the day, causing Salome's shoes to sink into the ground with each step. Large slippery roots surfaced from the base of the trees. David looked down at his phone. "This way," he said pointing further into the trees.

Salome was almost certain that his phone was wrong. Most of the area around where her employer lived was cultivated, and going further into the woods seemed like it was taking her further off track. "Are you sure?"

"Definitely, the GPS says to go this way. It's connected to a satellite in outer space. Do you know what space is?"

Salome laughed. "I'm Amish, not an idiot. Of course I know what space is. There's an American flag on the moon." She had seen the pictures in the library.

"Sorry," Dave said sheepishly. They walked a bit further, and the tree cover overhead grew thicker. Salome shivered. She wasn't sure how she felt about being alone with a stranger, a strange boy. Though David had been nothing but nice so far.

"How long have you and Mike been seeing each other?"

"About a month," Salome said. Her face flushed. She felt so stupid, imagining a future together with an *Englisch* boy who was practically a stranger, and then to find out in the worst, most embarrassing way that Mike had a girlfriend. She really was an idiot, Amish or not.

Dave stepped closer to her, uncomfortably in her space. His shoulder almost brushed hers. "Did you kiss a lot?"

Salome angled herself away from him. "I don't think that's your business."

"No offense." He waved his hands in front of him, his right still gripping the phone.

She could see the glinting of the sun through the trees. From where she was standing, and thinking of the time of day, the sun was more to the west, and they were following it almost parallel. They had to be going the wrong way. Mrs. Ashton's house was northeast of where the party had been.

"Can I see the phone?" She didn't exactly know how it worked, but she knew how to read a map.

"It's fine. I know where we are going," David snapped.

"Just let me see it."

"Give me a second."

Salome didn't like this. "I think I can make it from here. Don't worry about it. I know where I am."

"You do?" He sounded surprised.

"*Ja*," Salome said. It was a lie, but she hadn't sworn to follow the Ordnung yet, and she didn't even plan to, so she wouldn't let herself be upset about that. "You should go back. I'm okay."

David looked down at his phone. "I think I might've lost my signal. Can I go with you a bit more until I get it back?"

First he had known exactly where he was going, and now he seemed to have lost the signal on his phone and he still needed to follow her. He didn't necessarily mean anything sinister. He was probably just embarrassed that his device had failed him, but she still didn't like it. And she didn't like the questions he had asked, or the way he had stood so close and asked about her kissing his friend. At the same time, if he was lost, she didn't just want to leave him wandering around Lancaster by himself. That wasn't right either.

"Okay, you can come with me. But we're going back that

way." She pointed behind them. Once they were out of the tree cover, she would be able to see where she was going. Maybe she could go to one of the farmhouses and ask for directions. However it happened, she was in a lot of trouble. She would probably lose her job, which was her own fault. She never should have trusted that Mike would take her out for a half hour and bring her back. She never should have trusted Mike at all. "What time is it?"

He looked at the phone. "It's almost three."

Her stomach sank. Ms. Ashton would definitely be awake by 3:30. When she woke up, and Salome wasn't there, she would think the worst. And she would have a right to think that. But they weren't out of time yet. Salome picked up her skirt and walked faster.

"Slow down!" Dave said, jogging after her.

"I have to get back."

"Can't you just wait for one minute?"

Salome stopped for a second and looked back over the shoulder. It was at that point that Dave grabbed her arm.

"Let me go!" Salome shouted.

"Do you like American boys?"

What was he even talking about? "I said let me go."

"Mike and I are very good friends. We talked about you."

Salome tried to wrest herself from his grip, but he only squeezed tighter and pulled her to him. "I will let you go if you give me a kiss."

Salome's heart beat in her chest so loudly she could hear it in her ears. She was scared and also furious. At home, she had to grit her teeth, lower her gaze, and accept things as they were. And she saw what came from that. She saw how her *mamm* wasted away into a shadow of herself, her shoulders bowed under the weight of a household and a husband who loved himself more than he cared for his family.

Salome put up with things at home, but she wouldn't take it from a stranger—especially not a stranger who wanted things that she had no interest in giving. So with the strength of her anger, she shifted her weight, ramming her knee up into his crotch. He screamed, and in that instant, his grip loosened. Salome shoved him back and ran.

Behind her, Dave cursed. But she was running, her skirt lifted as she tore between the trees. She could see the field ahead of her. But the ground was still damp and in her haste, she tripped on one of the exposed roots. The damp ground did the rest. Between one step and the next, she was sprawled on the ground.

Dave grabbed her by the back of her dress. She screamed. And then, like an angel in the distance, silhouetted by the light in the break between two trees, she saw Beanpole.

"Help!" she screamed. "Beanpole!"

"Shut up!" David whispered and pulled her behind a tree. But it was too late. Beanpole had seen, and he ran at the pair of them, his expression a mask of fury.

"You'd better let Salome go," he shouted. In his right hand, he held a pick hoe.

>> Present Day

Susie woke in the hospital, the smell of bleach in her nose and a needle in her arm. She opened her eyes. They were gummy and dry. Tiffany stared down at her.

"Susie, you're awake? Good! Don't worry! Your baby's fine. It's a— Wait, you don't want to know. You were dehydrated and they put you on an IV. Can you say something?"

Behind Tiffany was a window overlooking the parking lot. A line of sun glare reflected from the metal windowpane, dazzling her vision for a second before she averted her gaze. "I'm in the hospital?" Joe was going to be furious. "My husband?" Was it awful that she was hoping Joe hadn't been called.

"I called Mister Zook at the number you gave me, and he said that he would make sure Joe got here as quickly as possible."

Susie blinked, clearing her vision. She was in an *Englisch* hospital, and a low beep sounded from some kind of machine on the wall behind her. "What happened?"

"You're not drinking enough. That's what the doctor said. You didn't notice you were thirsty? You're supposed to drink 8 to 10…no 12 glasses of water a day. Have you been sick?"

She had felt nauseous. And it had been difficult to eat last night. Mostly she moved the food around on her plate, her head pounding with anticipation for today's meeting. She hadn't even thought about it. "I'm sorry."

At that moment, the door to the hospital room opened and Joe, forehead glistening with sweat, ran in. He smelled of sawdust and home. And when he took her hand, the weight of guilt and the warmth of her love for him swept through her.

"What happened?" Joe asked, wiping his forehead with the sleeve of his free hand. "There's a police detective outside your door. He said you had fainted. What happened? Is the baby—?"

"Our *bobbeli* is fine," Susie managed to say.

"Let her take a breath," Tiffany cut in. "She's fine. Your baby is fine. Everything is going to be okay."

Susie nodded. She couldn't be more grateful that her friend was there.

"Why don't the two of you take some time? I'm going to get the nurse." Tiffany started toward the door. She gave Susie a reassuring smile as she left.

"Where were you? At the store?"

It was against the Ordnung to lie, and Susie had already been skirting the boundaries of that by not telling her husband what she had been doing. How she had been investigating what happened to Salome. It was time to come clean.

"I-I went to the police station in Lancaster to speak with Detective Martinez."

"Why?"

"He was one of the two detectives who investigated what happened when Salome ran away. I went to her house, and found a picture of her with three *Englisch* boys." Susie blinked rapidly. "Salome had a boyfriend—an *Englisch* boyfriend. And I think that one of his friends did something to her."

"You had a picture? A photograph? Where? Why didn't you tell me?"

"I know you didn't want me to talk to Beanpole anymore, and I haven't. But I don't think that Salome ran off. And Beanpole attacked…" Susie shook her head. "No, not attacked, he *grabbed* a girl by the arm the evening Salome disappeared, and he was acting crazy. She used something to break his hold that her brother had taught her, and then some of the other youth from the district came by, and nothing really happened, but I thought it meant something. So Tiffany and I went to Ephrata to find out what had happened—"

"You went to Ephrata. When? You have been going behind

my back all of this time?"

"I wasn't trying to lie. I just knew it would upset you."

"Of course it upsets me. You're carrying our child. And you are my wife. And you don't trust me."

"I trust you."

"If you trusted me, you would tell me the truth."

"I love you. And you know I would never do anything to endanger our child. Please, don't be angry." Susie sobbed. "I just... I know you don't understand, but Salome was my best friend. And that guy, Anderson, he's in jail for... Detective Martinez thinks he might have hurt Salome. Maybe that's why she hasn't come back." Or maybe it was something worse. That cold, jittery thought that Susie had been assiduously avoiding, "If I hadn't found that picture, detectives wouldn't know. I might have been wrong about Beanpole, but something happened to Salome. She didn't just leave."

Joe sighed. He squeezed her hand. "I know how much you cared for Salome. I don't want us to be at odds with each other. But you can't hide things from me. I don't hide things from you."

Susie nodded. It hurt, but her husband was right. "I never wanted to do anything to hurt our baby."

"Of course, I know that. But why couldn't you have said anything? I would've helped. I did help. I spoke with

Beanpole."

"I know. I'm sorry."

"Stop apologizing. I don't need you to apologize. I need to know that we are in this together. That's what we promised each other."

"We are. Maybe it was pride, or guilt, I don't know. I just can't let it go."

"Even if it kills our baby?"

Susie knew that he was just trying to make his point, but his words were like an ice pick in her chest. She couldn't breathe.

"Susie! I didn't mean that!"

"Is that what you think happened?" Two babies. Two innocent souls who had not even made it half as long as the little one she carried now. Both gone. Both her fault.

"*Ne!*"

"I've always asked myself, what if I had done more? Did I miss something? I know, and I'm here in the hospital now. I don't blame you for thinking that I—"

"I never thought that. I don't think that. And I know what you want to help your friend. You feel guilty about that too."

"I just feel like there has to be something I missed."

"If you did, that doesn't make it your fault. I know it's hard, and I want to help. But I also want us to have the life together that we both want."

Susie looked up into her husband's eyes. She could feel the warmth of his love for her, and she hoped he knew how much she loved him. "I want us to have a life together. Our baby. Everything. You don't know how much. Tiffany said that the doctor said the reason I passed out was dehydration. And I've just been so worried and upset. I should've been paying more attention. Tiffany gave me some water this morning, but I took a sip and it just made me feel sick. I thought I would be okay. I thought it was just that I was going to the station to see the detective and I was nervous, but I shouldn't have kept it from you."

"Promise me you will let this go now. You said it yourself, the police are handling it. Let them do their jobs."

Joe was right. Why should Susie think that anything she did would be more effective, better, than the work of a trained detective? Of course, it was ridiculous to think that she could do more.

There was a knock on her hospital room door, it opened, and a woman in a white lab coat walked in. "I'm Doctor Belmont," she said. "You probably don't remember me. You were unconscious. But we have regulated your electrolytes and gotten your fluids up. Your baby's placenta is also a bit lower than I would like, closer to the cervix, but we will monitor that. If we need to, we will do a cesarean section though hopefully you will be able to have a natural childbirth." She walked to the foot of Susie's bed and leafed through her records on the clipboard. "How have you been feeling? Your white blood cell count was a bit elevated, have you been having symptoms of nausea?"

"*Ja*—yes, for the past day or so. And I have had back pain. My mother said it was normal. And it was nothing like what happened when I miscarried before, but I should have been more cautious."

"Don't be too hard on yourself. It's possible you have a stomach virus, but things are sometimes collocated when you are pregnant." She smiled. "I want to send you home with some medication. Will you take it?"

Susie nodded. "Yes, doctor. I'll do what I need to. I want to have a healthy baby."

"Good. Sometimes, as women, we can work ourselves too hard and not even realize what is happening. It's important to pay attention to the signals that your body is giving you. And be gentle with yourself. You don't have to do everything."

Yes, her husband and the doctor were right. She needed to take better care of herself. She also had to what she needed to make sure that her baby came into the world healthy and strong.

Besides, if that *Englisch* boy had hurt Salome, he was in jail now. There was nothing else Susie could do about it. And yes,

Beanpole was strange, but even the girl that he had frightened said that he hadn't done anything to hurt her. And there was nothing else to indicate he had hurt anyone else either. With the evidence she had given the detective, maybe there would be enough to bring Salome out of hiding. Maybe she would testify. Maybe... She didn't know.

Either way, it was unlikely that Beanpole had anything to do with this. Not when there was already a convicted criminal who was with the group that Salome had supposedly run off with.

It is important not to theorize ahead of your evidence. Wasn't that what Detective Martinez had said? But it made sense that an outsider, one with violent tendencies, would have done something to Salome. It certainly made more sense than it being one of their own.

"I will take care of myself," Susie promised.

It was only later that night, standing in the bathroom taking the antibiotic that the doctor had prescribed for her that Susie realized she had not actually promised to stop investigating what happened to Salome.

Not that the detectives needed her help. God had sent her to find that picture and to guide Detective Martinez to the Englisher who had...who hopefully *had not* done anything. But if he had, was it that Salome was too ashamed to return? Maybe. And the worst of it was Susie had no way to find her friend if she didn't want to be found. The best she could hope was that Salome was happy, wherever she had ended up.

Dear God, let Salome be happy.

Though Susie knew that God answers all prayers, she did not feel at peace when she left the bathroom and returned to her husband's arms. There was nothing she could do, but at the same time, she couldn't escape the feeling that she had not done enough.

MISSING

CHAPTER TWELVE

>> Present Day

When Jumbo got back from his meeting with the psychiatrist, he opened the door to his home to shouting and the smell of stew. Both came from the kitchen. Jumbo quickly took off his coat and hung it on the hook by the door before walking briskly through the house and into what looked and sounded like a bitter fight between his wife and his son.

"…Stay faithful to Salome! She ran off, and thank God she did. That girl has possessed you!"

"Stop talking about her like that!"

Beanpole stood beside the sink, both of his hands balled into fists as he glared, red-faced at his mother. Emma was by the stove. A hot pot of stew bubbled beside her.

"What's going on?" Jumbo asked.

"Remember, *daed*," Beanpole said. "You agreed. I'm staying faithful to Salome. And she"—Beanpole pointed at his *mamm*—"She shouldn't talk about Salome that way."

Jumbo stepped forward, his hands out in front of him to try and calm his wife and son down. "Emma, I know you didn't mean anything by it."

"Don't put words in my mouth, Jumbo. I meant everything I said. That girl's father is polluted by the drink, and she came out twisted. There is an evil inside of her. And I won't have that evil touch my son."

"You're the one that's evil," Beanpole said. His voice was low and intense and he looked like he wanted to hit her.

"Is that what she's done to you? Made you disrespect your mother? Made you want to hurt me? Honor thy father and mother: and, he that curseth father or mother, let him die the death."

"Matthew 15:4," Beanpole shot back. "I know what the Bible says. It doesn't change that you have always hated me. And you hate her because she makes me happy."

"How could you say that?" Emma's hands were shaking. Without even putting on her oven mitt, she reached for the pot of stew. "You have the seed of sin inside of you, but God knows I've tried. I've given you everything. And yet you spurn me. You would set me aside for a girl who is even now fornicating with *Englischers*. This is how you repay me? I gave you life." She had the stew pot by both hands now. "I gave you life! I gave you food and shelter. I gave you the word of God. And now you tell me all of that is nothing. Cast me aside for a whore."

Jumbo's heart was pounding. His son was furious, and his wife was acting insane. "Put that down! Emma, please."

"Stay out of this, Jumbo. I'm doing God's work now. That girl has corrupted our son. Beanpole must be cleansed."

Her palms brushed the hot metal with the sizzle of burning flesh. She hurled the pot of boiling stew. Jumbo, terrified, slammed into his wife, praying he was able to stop the pot from hitting his son.

Beanpole stared, wide eyed, his expression frozen in shock and horror as the steaming, pot of hot stew flew through the air toward him. At the very last moment, Beanpole ducked, throwing his arms over his head. Stew splattered against his arms and the side of his face. He screamed.

Jumbo shoved Emma into the stove. The burner was still on, and her sleeve caught fire. She screamed, waving her arm in the air. Jumbo grabbed the oven mitt and smacked at the flame with it, putting the fire out.

On the floor, curled up, with his arms over his head, Beanpole sobbed.

"Beanpole!" Jumbo shouted.

His son looked up. Angry red splatters of broth dotted his temple and front of his left arm, though thanks be to God, most of it had missed and was splattered against the wall and cabinets behind him.

Jumbo said, "I need you to go to Mister Stoltzfus's barn and use his phone. You are going to call," Jumbo rattled off the psychiatrist's phone number from memory. "Get the pen and paper off the refrigerator and write that down."

"What are you doing, Jumbo?" Emma asked. Her voice had lost that sharp edge of fury. She sounded lost. "My arm, it hurts. I think I burned it on the stove."

"You did," Jumbo said. "And Beanpole is going to get you a doctor.

"Why is that pot of stew on the floor?"

"Beanpole, did you write down the number?"

Beanpole nodded. His gaze flitted between Emma and Jumbo.

"Good. When you get to the phone, call this number and tell him that your mother has had an episode. You can explain what happened. And tell him that she needs a doctor immediately. He will know what to do." Jumbo prayed that he would.

Until now, Jumbo had been able to look the other way. He hadn't seen what happened in the house when he was at work, and he was able to ignore all of the small signs, but not anymore. No matter how much he wanted to pretend that his home was a harmonious one, it wasn't, and he couldn't remember when it ever had been. He needed help. Emma needed help. And Beanpole, he needed help more than any of them.

"*Ja, daed,*" Beanpole agreed. He stood, and wiping his face with his sleeve, he jogged from the kitchen. Less than a minute later, he heard the sound of the front door opening and closing, and then Jumbo was left with his wife.

He looked down at her singed sleeve. "Can I see your arm?" Jumbo asked gently.

Emma nodded. She still looked confused. "It hurts…and my hands, too," she said in a soft voice.

Jumbo gently pulled the sleeve up. Her wrist and lower forearm was angry and red, with blisters on her palms and where fire had darkened the fabric most. "We should run that under cold water and put a teabag on it," Jumbo said. He led her to the sink and turned on the cold-water tap.

"Teabags are in the canister on top of the refrigerator," Emma said.

Jumbo blinked, the weight of his grief and failure settling over him. "I'm so sorry," he said.

"You should be," Emma responded with a hint of her usual snappish tone. "Why did you shove me while I was cooking?"

"Do you remember what happened?"

"I know you did something. You made me throw that stew. And I almost hit my son!"

How had he let things get so out of hand? It was his job as husband and father to take care of his wife and children. And somehow, instead, he let everything fall apart.

"I'm sorry," he said again. He was sorry, for all of it. He just prayed that at the end there would be room in God's infinite heart for forgiveness.

MISSING

RUTH PRICE & SARAH CARMICHAEL

CHAPTER THIRTEEN

>> Present Day

The smell of baking sweet rolls filled Susie's home with a cinnamon warm scent that put a smile in her heart as she sat in the living room, quilting with the Bishop's wife, Esther, and Esther's niece Mary who had graduated from their one-room schoolhouse three years after Susie. Esther was a wiry woman with jet-black hair with shocks of gray. She had faint lines around her eyes and mouth. Left to her own devices, she was constantly in motion, moving a needle or sorting things or simply tapping on her magnifying glass with her index finger, which she did when her hands were not occupied with something else. Mary, in contrast, was a round, jittery brunette who blushed easily.

It had been three days since Susie had returned home from the hospital, and Esther had organized it so that the other ladies brought food and kept her company through the afternoon. Through the open curtains, the day threatened rain. Heavy gray clouds hung like dirty cotton balls over the barn and fields. An even heavier silence seemed to press in on Susie's warm farmhouse from all ends, but inside was filled with bright conversation and laughter.

"These are lovely," Esther said, picking up one of the quilt squares that Salome had made. "There are of a different design from the rest on your baby quilt."

"They were Salome's."

Esther's green eyes widened. "Salome? Have you heard from her? Has she come back?"

"*Ne*," Susie said. "Nothing. But I've been thinking of her, maybe because the baby is soon to be born, and I visited her family's house. I admit, I was hoping that I might find something that had been overlooked. I know it was presumptive…"

"You two were so close." Esther placed a hand on Susie's shoulder. "To be honest, I never thought she would just disappear like that. I know it must've hurt you."

Susie looked down at the quilt. It had grown large now, and the squares that Salome had made did stand out from Susie's, but she felt it gave the quilt character. She wished Salome would be able to see it. "It's in the past."

"Did you find anything? I heard you had gone to the police

station to speak with one of the detectives who had looked into Salome's case."

Susie wasn't surprised that Esther knew this. Of course, gossiping was a sin, but as the Bishop's wife, it was important for Esther to keep up with what was going on in the community, and she took that responsibility very seriously. She was the kind of person that you could tell things to, and while she shared news, she never shared secrets.

"One of the *Englisch* boys that Salome was *acquainted* with is in jail. It's possible..." Susie didn't want to even admit the possibility of what could have happened. The thought that the stranger had put his hands on Salome, frightened her, or something worse, made Susie's stomach churn.

"I see." Esther looked down at her own quilt, a marriage gift for her niece, and started sewing quietly for about a minute.

"Have you heard yet what happened to Emma Miller?" Mary asked in a soft voice.

"Mary!" Esther snapped.

"Emma... Beanpole's *mamm*?" Susie froze, her needle pushed halfway through the fabric. "What happened?"

"She was..." Mary glanced at Esther who sighed and gave a brief nod. "Emma had to be taken to the hospital. They say it was stress."

"*Ja*, it's probably good that Mary said something," Esther

said with a sigh. "Not for the purpose of gossip, which there has been far too much of lately in regards to this situation." Esther gave Mary a sharp glare, causing the younger woman to bow her head and feign a fierce concentration on her sewing. "In case you are not feeling well enough to attend the Church service on Sunday, the bishop is going to make an announcement. She... She's ill. The responsibilities of maintaining her household became too much for her they think. She is being seen by psychiatrists at an *Englisch* mental health hospital."

She'd known that Beanpole was odd, but Emma? Then again, thinking of it, Susie wasn't surprised. Emma always kept to herself, and sometimes she said things that were odd. Like how God didn't like this, or wanted that, but not in the way that people usually said such things. And sometimes she would stop and listen to the silence, and then say something, often wholly unrelated and sometimes mean. It was also odd that none of her other children had stayed in the district. They'd gone away on *Rumspringa*; and, while some had taken their kneeling vows, none had returned for more than the briefest visits at Second Christmas.

"I know. It was a shock to all of us. But we are trying to hold back on the spread of gossip; it's all that everyone is really talking about, which is why my husband really wants to make an announcement to set everyone's mind at ease. I suspect you're the only one who actually hasn't heard of this, because you've been ill yourself."

"It was just dehydration, the doctor said." Susie had a large cup of lemon iced tea sitting on the coffee table, which she took sips of periodically as she had since she returned home.

"And we're very, very thankful. You just focus on staying well."

Susie nodded. Mary began talking animatedly about their new dog. Susie let the chatter wash over her, but she couldn't stop thinking of Beanpole's mother. Beanpole had always been odd as well, and maybe some of his mother's "illness" had also passed on to him. It was uncharitable think that, but Susie wondered. Either way, his life was more difficult than she had known. Maybe that's why he had fixated on Salome—like might have recognized like. Salome also had her secrets. Thinking of it that way, Beanpole seemed less sinister and more sympathetic.

They worked through much of the afternoon, and Susie was grateful for Esther and Mary's help preparing meals for the rest of the week and helping her to get a leg up on her cleaning in addition to making good progress on all of their quilts. A light drizzle had started to fall when Esther and Mary started packing up their work.

"Are you sure you're going to be all right here by yourself until your husband gets home?"

"*Ja*, I will." And as grateful as Susie was to have had them both take so much time from their own work to help her, Susie would also be glad to have a little time to herself once they left.

On Susie's first day back from the hospital, Joe had not even gone into the carpentry shop. He barely let Susie out of his sight, and Susie was pretty sure that if Esther and Mary hadn't arranged to come and visit today, Joe would have stayed home again.

The sound of a car engine coming up the driveway jogged Susie from her thoughts. Who would be arriving by car to see her tonight? Detective Martinez? A shiver passed through her. Was it something about Salome? Susie looked through the window toward the driveway, and that rush of anticipation and fear eased as she recognized Tiffany's car. Tiffany? It had to be. Susie pushed the quilt she was working on to the cushion of the sofa beside her and stood up.

Esther jumped to her feet. "You stay where you are. I can see who it is."

"It has to be Tiffany," Susie said. She didn't sit back down. After two days of everyone treating her as if she were made out of glass, she wanted to stand up and move around a little bit. She followed Esther to the door, though the older woman gave Susie a sharp look for doing so.

Esther pulled the door open, and both women looked out to see Tiffany crossing the driveway from her car and approaching the porch steps.

"Tiffany!" Susie exclaimed. She was relieved. She had been a bit worried that Tiffany might be nervous to visit after what happened when they went to the police station, even though she and Joe had assured her friend that of course she wanted to see Tiffany again.

"Susie, you're looking really great! Excuse me," Tiffany said, her gaze resting on Esther. "I didn't realize you had company. I don't want to impose…"

"*Ne*! You're not imposing! I'm happy you can visit!" Susie hoped she didn't sound too eager.

"Is this your *Englisch* friend?" Esther pulled the door open wide, and Susie stepped aside so that Tiffany could walk into the living room. "The one you were telling us about who sells houses?"

Susie nodded. "Tiffany and her husband, Malcolm, have been so wonderful to us."

Tiffany gave a shy smile. "I would've called ahead but…"

Susie laughed. "Tiffany, let me introduce Esther, the Bishop's wife and Mary, Esther's niece. They were helping me out around the house today."

"It's a pleasure," Tiffany said, shifting her box into her left hand and extending her right one. Esther shook it awkwardly. Tiffany said, "Whatever you guys were cooking, it smells wonderful. I guess you didn't need this, but I brought a pie. It's my grandmother's recipe—sweet potato, no crust."

Susie grinned. "That sounds delicious. Come on in. Esther and Mary were just packing up, and Joe should be back in about an hour. How's Malcolm?"

"He's doing well. He's been working late the past couple of weeks though."

"Mary, why don't you go and get the horse on the buggy?" Esther suggested.

Mary nodded and went to the hook to get her coat on.

Tiffany held out the pie box. "Should I put this in the kitchen?"

"*Ja*," Susie said. "There's room on the counter next to the stove."

The other two women had finished packing up their cookbook and bags as Tiffany came back into the living room.

"And the two of you will be fine alone until Joe gets back?" Esther asked.

"I promise," Susie said. "I'm feeling very good—normal actually—even with all the kicking."

"*Gutt*," Esther continued speaking in rapid-fire Pennsylvania Dutch. "The casserole is in the oven. After you and Joe finish your dinner, make certain to have him cover that with tinfoil and put it in the refrigerator. You shouldn't be lifting it."

"I really am feeling well."

"Don't worry," Tiffany said. "I'll take care of things."

Esther's eyes widened. "You speak Pennsylvania Dutch?"

"Not really. But I know that tone of voice. My mother gets the same way when she's giving orders and, well, mothering."

Esther laughed, and her shoulders seemed to relax. "Listen to your friend, Susie."

Susie and Tiffany walked Esther to the front door and waved as the two women got into their buggy and began to pull away.

"I should probably start getting dinner set for Joe and me," Susie said. "Did you want to stay?"

"No, I was just making a quick visit on my way home. Malcolm's supposed to be home before eight, so I thought we could order in."

"That sounds nice."

"But I can certainly help you get things together for you and Joe. And I hope you like the pie."

"I know we will. Can I get you something to drink? Tea, coffee?"

"I should be asking you that. You really are feeling okay?"

"Yes! Really, yes, I am."

Tiffany laughed. "I'm sorry. I know how it feels to be mollycoddled, though when you just passed out like that it was scary, really scary."

"I should have been taking better care of myself. But I am now. I feel like a fish, I've been drinking so much."

Tiffany laughed.

Susie and Tiffany got to work setting the table. As Susie laid down the silverware, Tiffany said, "I really don't want to bother you or anything, but I was hoping you might know something about the person who manages one of the properties near here. There's a farmhouse near Poplar Drive. It's about a mile from here. I know that it's not owned by anyone Amish, but the name of the property manager sounded like it could've been Amish. Andrew Miller Junior?"

A feeling of intense cold passed over Susie, and shocked, she could only stare. Nobody called either of the Andrew Millers by their actual names, so it wasn't surprising that even though Susie had spent a lot of time talking about Beanpole, Tiffany wouldn't recognize his Christian name. But Susie did. And she remembered the last time she had seen Beanpole near that area, clutching a paper bag full of red ribbons.

"Susie! Are you okay?"

Susie nodded. At that moment, her baby gave a flurry of fierce kicks. Susie rested her hand on her stomach.

"Are you sure? Does the baby feel okay?"

"*Ja*, I'm fine. I'll ask around about the property," Susie said. "Why do you need to speak with Andrew Miller?"

"I have a buyer for the property, but the phone number listed for the owner is out of service. I thought if I could get in contact with the property manager, he might be able to put me in touch with the owner. It's a really good offer."

Susie nodded. "I'll see what I can do to help."

She should have told Tiffany more, but the quiet feeling inside her said to keep it to herself. It was the same feeling that had led her to visit Salome's parents' home, and guided her to the photograph.

I need to go and look at the house.

No. That was the last thing she needed to do. Hadn't she already gotten herself into enough trouble?

But as much as she tried to convince herself to let it go, the thought haunted her through dinner and into the night, and Susie knew that she would go and see the house that Beanpole had been caring for—if only to prove herself wrong.

CHAPTER FOURTEEN

>> Present Day

Three days later, Susie took the buggy out to the house. It was sunny and unseasonably warm, and Susie fanned herself as she drove. She saw the break in the trees showing a narrow driveway leading away from the road. Susie took a sip from a thermos of iced tea on the driver's ledge beside her.

The driveway leading to the house was hard, packed dirt overgrown on each side with tall weeds. As far as property maintenance went, the weeds didn't inspire Susie, and as she turned her buggy up the driveway, she wondered how long it had been since the actual owner of the property had come to take a look at Beanpole's work. But as she approached the house itself, the grass on each side of her became neater and well trimmed and the land around the house was almost pristine with a vegetable garden in front, and a well maintained, white painted fence separating the yard around the house from the trees that surrounded it.

Susie pulled on the reins, slowing her pace and directing Star to the edge of the driveway where the dirt met the neatly trimmed grass.

She stepped out of the buggy into the sun. It was a perfectly ordinary looking house. For a moment, Susie questioned herself.

Why am I here?

But as she walked closer to the house, something seemed off. The house was freshly painted, but the concrete stairs leading up to the porch were chipped and uneven. A window to the basement had been boarded up.

Susie walked a slow circle around until she came to a tree. A chill passed over her. The tree was small, little more than a sapling, and in its spot behind the house, it had not been visible from the road. Hanging from its branches was a blaze of red. At first, she thought that the weeping trails might be the lingering remains of autumn leaves. But as the wind passed through them, they fluttered like thick strands of hair—they were ribbons.

Tens of dozens of them, some old and frayed in grayish brown while others were rust colored and others still a newer vibrant red. Susie walked to the tree and ran her fingers through the ribbons on the lowest branches. Her throat felt thick, and she wanted to cry. Why had Beanpole done this? It was like a memorial.

On the ground at the base of the tree was a flat white stone. Susie knelt and brushed her hand across it, as though she expected something, some writing, to become visible. But there was nothing engraved there. It was just a flat white stone, about a foot wide and 2 1/2 inches thick.

She looked up at the tree. Sunlight wove through the fluttering ribbons. A few withered leaves hung to the branches.

Tears caught in Susie's lashes. Her vision blurred.

Salome is dead.

She couldn't say the words out loud, but they felt real to her.

Dear *Gott*, let me be wrong about this.

But God didn't answer. Not in words she could hear nor feelings she could understand.

She was so caught up in her grief that she didn't hear Beanpole's footsteps until it was too late.

"Get off of her!" he shouted.

Susie wiped the tears from her eyes with her sleeve as she scrambled to her feet. It was Beanpole, running from the tree line and over the fence at her.

Susie screamed, "Stop!"

But Beanpole wasn't listening and he wasn't slowing down. In his right hand, he clutched a paper bag. Susie knew what was inside. And though she was afraid, she was also furious. "What did you do to her?" she demanded.

"I helped her! The *Englisch* boy was hurting her, and she called my name. She was an angel, and he was hurting her. I never wanted her to get hurt. We were going to get married. All I ever wanted was to make her happy."

"Then why did—? She's here, isn't she?" Susie pointed down at the base of the tree.

"There was so much blood—too much blood. I tried to stop it. I never wanted to hurt her. We were going to get married." Beanpole slowed down as he approached the tree. He and Susie stood on opposite sides of the stone. He opened the bag and took out a handful of perfectly cut ribbons. Reaching up, he tied one around the branch above him. "I brought you ribbons, see? Don't you like them?"

Susie took a step back. "What happened?"

"He was hurting her, so I hit him with the pick hoe. But he ran, and there was too much blood. Salome wouldn't wake up. I let her sleep, but she wouldn't wake, and I couldn't leave her there. So I took her home."

Emma, Beanpole's mother, had been taken away to a psychiatric hospital. And as far as Susie could tell, it seemed that Beanpole was also damaged.

He reached up and tied another ribbon on the tree branch. "I remember she said once that she wanted to wear red ribbons. It's not our way, but she should be allowed this." His shoulders heaved and he dropped to his knees. "I'm sorry. I'm so sorry."

Had he killed her? She wasn't even sure if she could trust his confession. Nor could she know if he would turn on her as he might have turned on Salome.

"I'm sorry to have bothered you," Susie said, backing away a step at a time from where she'd stood next to what Susie knew in her heart was her best friend's grave. "I should go."

"Please," he said. "Please, don't tell anyone what I did. I didn't mean it. You have to believe me! I never would have hurt her."

"I do believe you." And she did. But she did not make a promise not to tell. She would not leave her best friend buried in a stranger's yard in the care of her killer.

Tears streamed down Susie's face as she left, still sobbing and apologizing to the ghost of her friend.

EPILOGUE

>> Present Day

After Susie called Detective Martinez and explained what had happened, the police worked into the night. The next morning, they arrested Beanpole. He went with them without argument or struggle.

Jumbo watched as his son, like his wife, was taken away. Guilt crushed him like a vice, and he couldn't breathe. His chest hurt. He clutched it, wheezing, as everything around him blurred. Everything he'd done, everything he had ignored, every lie he'd told, he had done it for the benefit of his family. His hell had been paved with his own intentions, and he wanted to die of them.

"Mister Miller?" the detective asked.

"It was me."

"Excuse me?"

"All of it. It was my fault. Take me instead."

"I'm sorry," the detective with the kind brown eyes said. "We can't take on the sins of our children."

"All of his sins are mine."

"Be that as it may, your confession would not hold up in court."

Jumbo nodded. "Can I—? Can I go with him?"

"Not in the car, but one of the officers can give you a ride to the station. Your son will be kept there until bail is set. From everything Missus Zook told me, he never intended to kill the girl. His cooperation will be taken into account in combination with the forensic evidence."

"I didn't see Salome get in the car that day. I should have said something before, but I didn't see that," Jumbo said.

The detective nodded. "I will make a note of that."

"I should have known."

"Did your son ask you to hide his crime?"

"*Ne.*"

Beanpole hadn't asked him to hide anything. He never asked. But Jumbo had hidden things all the same.

>> Ten Years Ago

Salome laughed, her lips purplish red with berry juice. She and Susie were covered in it. Their bellies ached from the handfuls they had eaten, and now they lay side-by-side beneath the largest bush, which they had stripped clean for their baskets.

"Do you think your *mamm* will make pies?"

"*Ja*, and tarts, and bread. And she'll mix some in with some of the gravy for the chicken maybe, to give it color and make it sweet. You should come over for dinner and spend the night, if your *daed* says it's okay."

"He won't care." Salome sighed. They lay quietly for almost a minute, looking up at the sky, before Salome asked, "Suz, when you have a baby, what do you want to name him? Or her?"

"I don't know."

"If I have a girl, I'm going to name her Susannah. And I'll call her Susie, like you."

"And if I have a girl, I'll name her Salome."

"*Ne*, don't stick the poor girl with a name like Salome. Name her Margaret, like Captain America's girlfriend. You like Captain America, right?"

"Margaret's not an Amish name."

"Then make it her nickname. Or pick whatever name you

want. It'll be your baby." Salome sat up and shoved another handful of berries into her mouth. Then she stood and pointed to a tree stump in the distance. "Race you!"

As usual, Salome started running before Susie could get up. Susie jumped to her feet and followed with all of her strength. In the end, she reached out and almost caught her best friend's skirt before Salome leapt up onto the stump, strands of hair escaping her bonnet to fall in her eyes. She thrust her two baskets of berries into the air and shouted, "I win!"

"You always cheat. It's not fair!"

"Life's not fair, Susie. But win or lose, you'll always be my best friend."

"*Ja*, the same. Friends forever."

THE END.

Thank you for Reading!

I hope you enjoyed reading this as much as I loved writing it! If so, you can find more of my work where eBooks and Paperback books are sold online.

Would you like to see more Amish mysteries with these characters? If so, drop me a line at ruth.price@globalgrafxpress.com and let me and Sarah know.

Also, for a LIMITED TIME, I am offering FIVE of my books for FREE digital download in my Starter Library.

Just visit

FamilyChristianBookstore.net/Ruth-Starter

Or send via TEXT MESSAGE

READRUTHPRICE to 1 (678) 506-7543

to get the Starter Library and updates from me. You can also find more of my work at FamilyChristianBookstore.net.

Lastly, if you enjoyed this book and want to continue to support our writing, please leave a review to let everyone know what you thought of this book. It's the best thing you can do to keep indie authors like me writing. (And if you find something in the book that – YIKES – makes you think it deserves less than 5-stars, drop me a line at ruth.price@globalgrafxpress.com and I'll fix it if I can.)

All the best,

Ruth and Sarah

AN AMISH COUNTRY TREASURE

An Amish girl. An Englisch reporter. A million dollar love story.

CHAPTER ONE

"Wait -- Jemima!"

Jemima King turned her head, but it was more out of habit than a real need to identify the voice. She would've known the sound of Mark Christner's voice in her sleep. They had lived next door to each other in the same Lancaster County community for 17 years.

He came running up and then stopped dead in the road. He bent double, caught his breath and laughed.

Jemima turned her eyes down demurely. Mark was always

at her elbow these days. There was nothing new about that – they were childhood playmates – but Mark's reasons were different now.

She stole a glance at him through her lashes.

Mark was no longer the scruffy little boy of her childhood, and that was especially clear on a day like this one, when the sun gave his black hair a silky blue sheen, and made the curve of his cheek look as downy and smooth as a peach.

He was almost as tall as her father now. And his voice was nearly as deep. Jemima pinched in a smile. She would have to be made of stone not to notice that Mark had filled out nicely – especially when he flashed those beautiful white teeth in her direction.

She looked down at her feet. Their relationship was changing fast. The same Mark who had once irritated and teased her was – strangely -- becoming more solicitous by the day.

Maybe that was because *she* had changed, too.

Mark used to tease her about her red hair and green eyes. He had said she looked like an orange cat, and had made her cry.

But just the other day Mark had compared her hair to a maple leaf in the fall, and her eyes to the color of sunshine through leaves.

"I'll walk you home," he volunteered, and put a big brown

hand out for her books.

Jemima smiled and gave them to him.

"What are you going to do, now that we've finished school? What are you going to do on *your* rumspringa, Mark?" she teased him. "Are you going to dress in English clothes and turn all the girls' heads?"

He grimaced wryly, and shook his head. "I'd just as soon dress up in a monkey suit," he said bluntly, and Jemima laughed outright.

"I'm disappointed in you, Mark," she said mischievously. "I was hoping you'd shock us all!"

Jemima enjoyed his chagrined expression out of her corner of her eye. She really shouldn't tease him, but it was *so* tempting. Mark was so *easy* to tease. No one she knew was more staunchly Amish, or more conservative. Mark reminded her of something big and strong and immovable, like the face of a mountain.

Or, maybe, *dormant volcano* would be a better description.

Because underneath all that unyielding rock, there was definitely warmth on the inside. She glanced at him affectionately then tilted her head, considering.

Maybe there was even a little *lava* under that mountain. She had seen one or two things lately that...

"Jemima, slow down!"

Jemima came back to herself. She stopped walking and turned around. Her little sister Deborah had fallen behind again, and was trotting along the dirt road to catch up.

"You… never… *wait for me*," Deborah complained, as she huffed along. She finally caught up with them and bent over double, gasping for breath.

Jemima looked at her little sister pityingly. Deborah's sandy brown hair had worked its way out from under her cap and was flying all around her face like a swarm of gnats.

She couldn't keep her hands from reaching out to smooth it back again. "Mind your hair, Deborah," she said softly.

Deborah swatted her hands away irritably. "I know how I look!" she snapped. "Maybe it's because I had to run! Next time just *wait* for me, and we can *both* look good!"

"That's no way to talk to your sis, Debby," Mark chided gently.

Deborah said nothing, but shot him a look that said, *Oh, shut up* as clearly as any words.

Jemima sighed and turned to him. "Never mind her, Mark, she has the temper of a wildcat. I know she doesn't mean half the things she says."

"I do, too – I mean *every word!*" Deborah countered, "Why shouldn't I, when you leave me behind to *flirt with your boyfriends*?"

"Debby!" cried Jemima and Mark, together.

"Oh, just forget it," Deborah fumed, "I'll walk home by myself. That's what you two *want*, anyway!" She hoisted her books up in her arms and stumped off, muttering under her breath.

Jemima shot Mark an apologetic look. "You'll have to forgive her, Mark," she explained, "Deborah's at that awkward stage. I'm sure that once it's over, she won't be – mad *all the time.*"

Mark tilted his head and watched Deborah as she disappeared down the road. "I don't remember *you* ever being that –" He cleared his throat and quickly amended, "I mean, I don't remember that *you* ever had a… hard time."

Jemima shook her head. "She's driving poor Mamm to despair. It's only a few years until Debby comes of age, and the way she's treating all the boys she knows, not one of them is going to court with her!"

"Well, at least your Mamm will never have that problem with *you*." Mark looked at her with transparent admiration, and she blushed.

They rounded a corner and the King homestead gradually moved into view. It was a large, white, two story house surrounded by several outbuildings, including the blacksmith shop where Jemima's father worked. Even from that distance, the faint sound of a hammer rang out over the fields.

There was a buggy parked at the front of the house, and Mark's dark eyebrows moved together. He shaded his eyes with one hand.

"Whose buggy is that?" he frowned.

Jemima looked at him uncomfortably. "It's probably Samuel Kauffman's," she murmured. "He said he'd be coming by this afternoon. His mother is sending Mamm some canning supplies."

Mark grunted suspiciously, and it was clear that he thought that Samuel Kauffman's mission was not primarily about preserving fruits and vegetables.

"Well, that sounds about right," he growled. "Samuel and your mamm are probably *trading recipes*."

"Mark!"

CHAPTER TWO

By the time they reached the front yard, it was clear that Samuel Kauffman was in attendance. His tall, slim frame was draped easily over one of the porch rails.

Samuel would have been at home at any beach in the world. He had a shock of bushy blond hair, he was brown as a nut, and his eyes were a sparkling blue. He greeted Jemima with a beautiful white smile and a wink that made her lower her eyes and go pink.

He acknowledged Mark with a cheery: "Well, look who's here! Sit down, Mark, you look exhausted. Can I get you a glass of water?"

Mark gave him a grim look, but replied: "I know you're *used* to doing that, but no thanks. We aren't at your folks' restaurant. Speaking of that – isn't it about time for you to put on your *apron*? It's getting close to dinner."

Jemima broke in hastily. "Samuel, it was very kind of you to come all the way out here. I'm sure Mamm appreciates it."

Samuel beamed at her. "It's nothing, Jemima. Anytime! I'm always happy to do what I can."

"*That's for sure*," Mark mumbled under his breath.

Jemima's eyes moved uncertainly between the two of them. "Would the two of you like to – to stay to supper?" she ventured.

"Can't," Samuel lamented, and reached out to take her hand. "But give me a rain check, okay? I'd love to see you some *other* time."

Jemima noticed, with trepidation, that Mark's brow was gathering thunder, and he looked as if he was about to burst out with the accompanying lightning. So she hurried to reply, "Oh, I'm sorry you can't stay with us, Samuel. But yes, do drop by when you can," she smiled.

Samuel squeezed her hand and ran his thumb over her palm in a way that made it tingle. Then he smiled, bounded down the porch steps, and was driving away before she found the nerve to look up.

Mark watched him go with a scowl. "Why do you encourage that skinny little weasel?" he blurted.

Jemima went red. "Samuel is a very good person -- and you know it, Mark Christner!" she retorted indignantly. "I don't know *why* you take such a dislike to him, but he doesn't deserve it."

Mark turned to look at her, and his blue eyes were sad and reproachful. "Don't you, Jemima?" he asked softly.

Jemima couldn't meet his eyes, and felt her cheeks going hot. But she was spared the necessity of a reply by the sound of her father's heavy shoes approaching on the gravel drive. His booming voice cut off any possibility of a reply.

"Jemima, shouldn't you be helping your mamm with dinner?" he said pointedly, and directed a speaking look at Mark.

Mark's cheeks went a dull red. Jemima nodded, gave her visitor an apologetic look, and fled.

After she had gone, the six-foot-three Jacob King leaned against one of the porch posts and regarded his 17-year-old guest with a knowing look in his eye.

"How is your family, Mark?" he inquired gently.

"They're fine, sir," Mark mumbled.

Jacob nodded. "Good. I haven't seen much of them lately. Or of *you*, for that matter."

Mark looked out across the fields and bit his lip.

"And that's *not* good," Jacob sighed, running a massive hand through his rumpled red hair. "Because if a young man comes to this house to see my daughter, I expect him to come to see me *first*."

"Yes, sir."

"Just so long as we understand one another," Jacob smiled, and clapped his hand down on Mark's shoulder – hard.

Mark winced, but nodded.

Jacob smiled. "Staying to supper, boy?" he inquired gently.

"Ah – no. I have chores to do."

"Say hello to your folks for me," Jacob told him, and stood on the porch, watching, until Mark Christner's retreating form disappeared down the long dirt road.

Jacob King put both hands on his hips and laughed long and loud, and then turned and entered his house.

His wife Rachel was waiting for him at the door, with her arms crossed. "Jacob King, you should be ashamed of yourself," she chided gently. "Jemima is finished with her schooling now. It's *time* for her to be getting visits from young men. And Mark is her… *special friend*. He's plainly working up the nerve to ask if he can court with her. Why do you discourage him? Don't you *want* your daughter to find a good husband?"

Jacob leaned over and kissed his wife's pretty pink cheek. "You can set your mind at rest, Rachel," he assured her, "we'll never have to worry that Jemima will *lose* a man. Her danger is going to be picking the right one, out of the teeming horde!"

"Jacob, what a way to put it!" his wife exclaimed, but her lips curled up a little. "It's true that Jemima is *very* blessed, but how will she ever know which of her suitors is right for her, if she never gets a chance to spend time with them?"

Jacob sighed, and stretched his rippling arms. "Don't tire me with those silly pups, Rachel," he yawned. "I'm *hungry*. I've spent all day hammering over a forge, and I could eat a horse."

"Come to dinner then, Jacob," she smiled softly. "The table is laid."

Jacob's eyes lighted on a large cardboard box sitting on one of the dining room chairs. He lifted a canning jar.

"What's this?"

His wife assumed an innocent look, and shrugged. "Samuel Kauffman came by this afternoon to bring me some jars. It was a gift from his mother."

"Oh, *did* he now?"

Jacob met his wife's eyes, and raised his brows comically. She looked away, and pinched in a smile.

"Your dinner is getting cold."

Jacob sat down at the groaning dinner table, and rubbed his hands. But before his family bowed their heads to pray, he gave his pretty daughter a meaningful look.

"Jemima, the next time you see Samuel Kauffman, tell him *I'd like a word with him.*"

"Oh, Daed!" Jemima gave him a pleading look from her lovely eyes, but her father was the one male on earth who had found the strength to resist it.

"I mean it."

CHAPTER THREE

"You're so *lucky,* Mima," Ruth Yoder sighed. "I wish I had *your* problems."

The next afternoon, Jemima and her best friend were sitting in the woods just beyond the family garden, and were talking *boys*.

Jemima's friend rested her chin on her hands and raised impish blue eyes to the sky. "*Oh, Mark, stop it,*" she simpered. "*Samuel, you'll make me cry!*"

Jemima rolled her eyes. "If you say that again with a big scowl on your face, you'll sound almost like Debby," she sighed. "Does *everybody* hate me, then?"

Ruth giggled and relented. "Of course not, Mima. Everybody *loves* you. All the boys do, anyway, and the girls just wish they *were* you!"

Jemima eyed her friend ruefully. "I wish they didn't," she confessed.

"Why not?" Ruth replied, stretching luxuriantly. She looked up at the sky through the tree branches. "If you've *got* it, *flaunt* it, I say. I just wish *I* had it, so I could *flaunt* it, too!"

Jemima giggled, and then hushed her. "*Quiet*, Ruth! Be careful what you say! Debby is hanging around somewhere, and if she hears you, you'll find yourself having to explain to your parents! I love my sister, but she's the biggest tattletale – "

A rustling in the bushes, about a stone's throw away, make Jemima break off. Sure enough, Deborah's scowling face materialized out of the leaves.

"So that's where you're hiding! Mamm says come and help her with lunch, Jemima. And you, too, Ruth -- *since you're here!*" Debby added rudely, and stalked off.

Jemima went red with embarrassment. She turned to her friend apologetically. "I'm sorry, Ruth," she stammered, "she's just so... *mean* these days. I don't know what's come over her!"

Ruth stood up, brushing grass from her skirt. "*I* do!" she replied tartly. She looked at Jemima's distressed face and bit back the rest of what she'd been planning to say. "But I'll be glad to help *you* with lunch."

Jemima clasped her friend's arm warmly. "*Of course* you'll

stay and eat with us," she pressed, and Ruth's expression relaxed. She nodded.

They hugged one another, and walked back to the house arm in arm.

But while they were in the kitchen, dutifully making sandwiches, there was a jaunty knock at the front door.

Samuel Kauffman stuck his head into the living room and smiled. "Knock knock! Is anybody home?"

"Why, Samuel," Rachel King exclaimed in a pleased tone, "come in! I hope everything is well with your folks?"

"They're fine," Samuel smiled.

The girls craned their necks to sneak a look at Samuel as he began to chat with Jemima's mother. Samuel towered over her, and he had taken his hat off in deference. His blond hair shone like summer wheat.

Ruth squeezed Jemima's arm in excitement, and they both smothered giggles.

"He's here to see you – lucky thing!" Ruth hissed.

Jemima blushed and smoothed her hair back, but to her consternation, her mother was saying:

"Well, Samuel, in that case, you'll have to go out to the shop and talk to Jacob. He won't let you court with Jemima unless you talk to him first."

Ruth hissed, "Did you hear that?"

Jemima put her hands over her mouth, and her heart began to beat oddly. She stopped even pretending to make sandwiches and inclined her ear to catch every word spoken.

"Thank you, Rachel," Samuel said in a respectful tone, and took his leave.

After the door closed behind him, Jemima's mother returned to the kitchen. She was trying hard to project a calm demeanor, but Jemima could see at once that her mother was on fire with excitement.

Jemima's eyes went to her mother's face. She searched it silently.

Rachel King broke down. "He wants to *court* with you, Jemima," she said thrillingly. "The second boy in as many *days*! Your father will be –"

But another quick knock at the door interrupted her words. They all turned to look through the kitchen door.

Another young man stood hat in hand on the doorstep.

Jemima looked at her mother worriedly. Her admirers were dropping by so often now that it was becoming almost *awkward*.

Rachel King took a deep breath, smoothed her apron, and went back out to greet their newest guest.

That evening at dinner, Jacob King put a forkful of potatoes into his mouth, and gave his lovely daughter a rueful glance.

"*Four* now," he told her, and Jemima turned a guilty red.

He turned to his wife. "What am I going to do with her?" he asked, with a twinkle in his eye. "If this keeps up, we're going to have to make them take *numbers*. I thought Samuel Kauffman and that what's-his-name Beiler boy were going to fight each other on the porch today."

Rachel smiled at Jemima. "Jemima is a *very* blessed young lady," she murmured happily. "Jemima, you should be praying every day for wisdom. You have an… unusual choice ahead of you. It isn't many girls who have so many suitors to choose from."

Deborah had been listening to the conversation in unhappy silence, but apparently she had endured her limit. She twisted her freckled face into a scowl and cried: "Jemima, Jemima, *Jemima*! If I hear one more word about *Jemima* and her *boyfriends*, I'm going to *throw up!*" She jumped up, flounced out of the room, and slammed the door behind her.

Jacob watched her, and frowned, but didn't seem disposed to interrupt his meal. He took another bite of ham. "Do you want me to get involved?" he asked quietly, and looked at his wife.

Rachel closed her eyes, but shook her head. "No. I'll take

care of it. I know what it is. She's going through an awkward phase, and the boys at school tease her. It's hard for her, and then to be compared to Jemima -- But I *can't wait* until she's fourteen, and over this – this –" She gave a soft huff, rose, and followed her daughter.

That left Jemima alone with her father. She raised her eyes tentatively to his face.

His expression softened as he looked down at her. "Well, Mima, you've got all the boys in this county rushing to my door! Got any that you want me to throw *back*?"

He winked and laughed, and Jemima blushed and sputtered, "Oh, *Daed*."

After dinner, Jemima went up to her bedroom and sat at the window. She brushed her glowing hair and looked out through the green curtain of trees. The window was open and a cool breath of air, smelling of mown grass, wafted in.

She really should be putting the finishing touches on her work. She had sewn three big boxes full of dolls to sell at the store in town. There was a big summer festival planned for the next morning, and she was going to have to get up early to get them to town before the shop opened.

Jemima sighed and looked down at the neatly stitched cloth dolls. There was a blank space where their faces would have been, as was Amish tradition.

She looked out through the trees again. She felt like a doll sometimes herself, only uncomfortably different – like the one *painted* doll in a box full of normal ones.

She put the brush down and sighed.

She couldn't concentrate on even the simplest task these days.

If she stared out the window long enough, she began to see faces – Mark Christner's strong face, and Samuel Kauffman's laughing one, and even Joseph Beiler's shy eyes.

Mark was strong and sure and steady and handsome and she knew him so well and was so comfortable with him.

Samuel was fun and easy to talk to and he made her laugh and he was always interesting.

Joseph was quiet and shy, but so handsome, and, she thought -- *very* smitten.

How could she choose between them? She couldn't bear the thought of hurting Mark -- *or* Samuel. And Joseph was so sweet and quiet.

She looked up at the soft twilit sky. Lord, what should I do? she prayed. I wouldn't hurt any of them for the world, but I'll have to, if I choose one over the others. Please show me what You want me to do.

She glanced back over her shoulder. She could hear the muffled sound of Deborah making noise in her own bedroom, across the hall. It sounded like she was muttering angrily and kicking something.

And please give me patience with Debby, Lord. Sometimes I have un-Christian thoughts about her.

There was a crash, and what sounded like a curse word, from across the hall. Then Deborah shrieked out, removing any doubt. There was a thunderous stomping sound, and Jemima's door burst open to reveal her angry sister.

"*Why* didn't you tell me that this clock you gave me was a piece of junk?" she demanded, throwing it down on Jemima's bed. "It just fell apart! I'm *tired* of getting all *your* old hand-me –"

Their mother appeared suddenly in the hall, her anxious eyes on Deborah's scowling face. "Deborah, that's no way to talk to your sister. I won't have you behaving like this. Go back to your room."

Deborah pinched her lips together and stomped out again.

Jemima met her mother's eyes ruefully, and they exchanged an unspoken comment before Rachel King sighed and closed Jemima's door after her.

Jemima turned to her work and closed up the big cardboard boxes. Then she turned down the lamp and undressed for bed.

Tomorrow morning was going to start early...

Thank you for Reading!

I hope you enjoyed reading this as much as I loved writing it! If so, you can find An Amish Country Treasures where eBooks and Paperback books are sold online.

Also, for a LIMITED TIME, I am offering FIVE of my books for FREE digital download in my Starter Library.

Just visit

FamilyChristianBookstore.net/Ruth-Starter

Or send via TEXT MESSAGE

READRUTHPRICE to 1 (678) 506-7543

to get the Starter Library and updates from me. You can also find more of my work at FamilyChristianBookstore.net.

Lastly, if you enjoyed this book and want to continue to support my writing, please leave me a review to let everyone know what you thought of my work. It's the best thing you can do to keep indie authors like me writing. (And if you find something in the book that – YIKES – makes you think it deserves less than 5-stars, drop me a line at ruth.price@globalgrafxpress.com and I'll fix it if I can.)

All the best,

Ruth

ABOUT THE AUTHORS

Ruth Price is a Pennsylvania native and devoted mother of four. After her youngest set off for college, she decided it was time to pursue her childhood dream to become a fiction writer. Drawing inspiration from her faith, her husband and love of her life Harold, and deep interest in Amish culture that stemmed from a childhood summer spent with her family on a Lancaster farm, Ruth began to pen the stories that had always jabbered away in her mind. Ruth believes that art at its best channels a higher good, and while she doesn't always reach that ideal, she hopes that her readers are entertained and inspired by her stories.

Sarah Carmichael has always loved telling stories, and when she met Ruth at a local farmer's market and the subject of writing came up, a friendship was born. Ruth and Sarah brainstormed intensively on Ruth's Yule Goat Calamity series, and worked together on The Long Run series and others. Through this collaboration, Sarah has also gained the confidence to start working on books on her own, which she will be publishing in the future. In her writing, Sarah strives to tell an entertaining story that shows the beauty of God through the seemingly small moments of our everyday lives.

You can keep up with Ruth and Sarah's new releases, discounts and specials and for a **LIMITED TIME GET 5 OF RUTH'S BOOKS EMAILED TO YOU FOR FREE as a part of Ruth's Starter Library**.

Grab it here at:

FamilyChristianBookstore.net/Ruth-Starter

Or get it via TEXT MESSAGE when you text READRUTHPRICE to 1 (678) 506-7543.